An
Ideal
Vessel

An Ideal Vessel is published by Dragon's Roost Press.

Material originally appeared in *The Crimson Pact* volumes 1,2&4

Printed in the United States of America
First Printing, 2018

ISBN-13: 978-0-9988878-3-8
ISBN-10: 0-9988878-3-8

Dragon's Roost Press
207 Gardendale
Ferndale, MI 48220

http://thedragonsroost.net/styled-3/index.html

2018

An Ideal Vessel

by Sarah Hans

DEDICATION

To the Writeshop,
fine writers and even better friends

PART 1

Elspeth

The vessel is perfect, but I am wary. I have traversed the void a thousand times, forcing myself into the bodies of those who will allow it, and never have I encountered such an excellent hollow specimen. Sometimes in desperation I have possessed children or animals, whose lack of strong personalities make it easy to take over their bodies. But always, in the end, they push me out, for the original personality cannot be removed, and can only be subsumed for a time. I struggle to maintain control of the physical form, and in the end I am always expelled.

Corpses are obviously easier to inhabit, but possessing a corpse is less ideal than it sounds. The body's functions no longer work, and I find it nearly impossible to move, or speak, or use any of the five senses properly. In the end, possessing a corpse is rather like being trapped in a cold, dark coffin, and without a personality there to expel me, I wonder perversely whether I would become permanently affixed in the dead body.

There are those who hover in the middle, however: the comatose, the brain-dead, people who were deprived of breath while being birthed. They are adults, with adult bodies, but lacking the mental faculties of an adult. I can possess them more easily and maintain control for longer, and I have little guilt if the body is destroyed in one battle or another; for what is a glorious death fighting the war against ultimate evil compared to a life of drooling misery?

But this vessel is something new. Even in those with limited mental acuity, the personality is still there, it is just dulled and unformed, like a knife freshly forged but not yet hammered or sharpened. This is an emptiness I do not understand, but I haven't the time to ponder it. The longer I linger without form, the more difficult it will be to remain on this plane, and I have a war to fight. I repeat the vow I once whispered by my dying lips as I swoop in to inhabit the vessel, throwing myself once more back into the fray.

Zuzanna

Zuzanna is the only worker willing to
stay past midnight, once again, and she takes up
sweeping with her usual methodical calm. She
secretly enjoys the Electricity Building at night,
when it is empty of visitors, and the only sounds
are the soft click of her shoes, the thrum of the
generators in the next room, and the susurrus of
the broom doing its work. Sometimes she hums
softly to herself, unable to remember the words
to the songs her mother used to sing her as a girl;
she has lost all the Russian she knew as a child,
but the sweetness of her mother's voice has never
left her.

She thinks she hears a sound under her
humming but doesn't stop. Mice sometimes
shuffle around in the dark, looking for scraps of
food the broom might have missed, and Zuzanna
has grown accustomed to their tiny sounds.

She takes especial care sweeping around
the stage. Children like to stand close to the
automatons, inevitably dropping popcorn and
peanuts in the cracks between the floor-boards.
The other women who clean the Electricity

Building curse the children and their careless parents, but Zuzanna thinks their carelessness is a sign of the exhibit's success. Professor Campion's Clockwork Automatons is by far the most popular exhibit in the Fair's programme, and she is honored that Professor Campion himself has chosen her and a few other lucky women to clean the rooms inhabited by his elegant creations. It is perhaps the closest she will ever come to fame or fortune.

She finishes sweeping and puts the broom and dustpan back in the closet. She considers dusting, but her arms are sore and she longs for the cold comfort of the bed in her rented room a few blocks from Jackson Park. No one will know if she neglects this duty for one night, so she unties her apron and hangs it on a peg inside the closet door. There is a mirror hanging just above the peg, and she catches her own reflection with a sigh. The hard work of the Fair is beginning to wear on her; she has dark circles under her eyes, lines around her mouth, and her expression is weary. She is no longer the rosy-cheeked idealist who came to Chicago looking for work as a shop girl, who ended up instead cleaning

the Electricity Building at the Columbian
World's Fair, working for a pittance and living
in a draughty rented room, still unmarried, still
unsuccessful by every measure.

Not for the first time, she wonders
what she will do when the Fair ends. She has
no prospects beyond sweeping the floors of this
temporary structure. She and thousands of others
will be without work, and competition for jobs
will be fierce. She dreads the thought that she
might have to work in a factory, like her mother,
breathing the sooty air until her lungs grow
tumors and stop her breath. She is too weary not
to think about the future that is just a few short
months away, and tears bubble from her eyes
before she can stop them.

Zuzanna is leaning against the closet
door, weeping softly, when she hears the sound
again. This time it is louder, more persistent, and
she realizes that someone must be in the building
with her. She grabs the broom and prepares to
defend herself, hoping that the intruder is not the
handsome Professor Campion, who will see her
exhausted, eyes swollen with weeping.

The curtain on the stage twitches.

"Who goes there?" Zuzanna cries, trying to sound intimidating. "Come out this instant!" Her voice cracks with fear. She brandishes the broom like a weapon.

The curtain parts gently. One of Professor Campion's automatons steps out from behind it, her wide eyes regarding Zuzanna, empty and expressionless. The mouth moves and a tinny voice says, "I'm so sorry, I didn't mean to frighten. Could you tell me where I am?"

Zuzanna swoons, her knees buckling. She collapses to the floor, dropping the broom with a clatter. The automaton moves to the edge of the stage, her motions stuttering and jerky, inhuman. Zuzanna watches her with horrified eyes; she is the prettiest and most human of the automatons, the only one whose skin is not metal, though her beige flesh still has an unnatural sheen. She has lustrous red hair that Zuzanna has often admired, and huge glass eyes with irises the color of emeralds. She is lovely, but she is still a mechanical thing, and should not be moving or speaking of her own accord.

As the creature climbs down the stage, Zuzanna screams and scrambles across the floor, trying to escape. One of her boots catches on her skirt and tears the fabric with a loud ripping sound, but she doesn't stop her terrified crab walk. Finally she backs into the wall beside the closet, where she turns her face away from the mechanical woman, hoping that either she or it will disappear.

"I am so sorry," the automaton says, still approaching. "I must be monstrous for you to react this way. I did not know."

Zuzanna spares a glance at the creature. She—It?—Is standing a few feet away, hands out in a gesture of innocence, eyes wider than ever. Zuzanna wonders whether she has finally worked too long and hard and suffered an hysterical breakdown. There seems to be no other explanation. How can this mechanical creature be speaking anything other than the words programmed for the exhibit? How can it be moving away from the stage, standing over her with that perpetually blank expression? But no matter how many times she tells herself that she must be mad, the walking, talking automaton refuses to disappear or return to her position on the stage.

Zuzanna sighs, and decides to accept her madness. Perhaps if she indulges this insanity it will pass.

"I'm sorry," she tells the automaton, her own voice sounding wooden and insincere. "You surprised me."

The creature breathes an audible sigh of relief—but how can it, without lungs?—and lowers her hands. "No, no, I am sorry. The urgency of my situation overwhelmed by good sense. Please, forgive me."

She looks up, apparently catching her reflection in the mirror hanging on the back of the open closet door. She moves awkwardly to the door, her movements jerky like those of a toddler just learning to walk, and stares at her reflection for several seconds. Then she makes a strange sound and says, "I'm a woman."

Zuzanna chortles. "You're not a woman, you're an automaton: Made to look like a woman, but not flesh and blood."

The automaton turns to look at her, huge eyes gleaming in the bright electric light of the closet. "Automaton?" she repeats.

Untangling her skirt from her boot,

Zuzanna rises and points to the banner over the stage, reading the words printed in huge letters: "Professor Campion's Clockwork Automatons, featuring Elspeth. That's you, you're Elspeth, the most lifelike automaton ever built. But still a mechanical thing, not living." Zuzanna takes some perverse pleasure in telling this perfect creature, with her shimmering skin and sparkling eyes, that she is not, in fact, a living being.

"But that's not possible," Elspeth says, her monotone voice somehow containing confusion.

Zuzanna shrugs. "You're right. You're only supposed to sing a song, say the words the Professor has given you to speak, do the motions he's dictated for you. But here you are, talking and walking and breathing!" As she speaks, she gestures ever more wildly, her voice gaining volume and pitch until it rings in her own ears.

"Oh dear," Elspeth says, her lovely red mouth making a round "o" of surprise. "That's why you were so frightened. You must think you're going mad. Oh my dear woman, I can assure you that's not the case. You are quite sane. Only—this should not have happened at all. Something is wrong."

The mechanical woman gazes up at the banner and then back at Zuzanna. "This Professor . . ."

"Campion."

"Campion. I should speak with him. I need to know how I came to inhabit this automaton."

"And how do you intend to do that? It's midnight. Everyone's gone home except the maids and security guards."

Elspeth clasps her hands, and it is such a human gesture of desperation that it sends a shiver across Zuzanna's skin. "Please, you must have some idea of how to contact him. It is incredibly urgent."

Zuzanna thinks longingly of her bed. But how can she abandon this pitiful creature? Elspeth's huge eyes and smooth skin remind her of someone she once loved, and ultimately it is that association that drives Zuzanna to say, "There is a place where the architects gather each night. If we're lucky, Professor Campion is there."

Elspeth looks as if she would cry with relief, if she had tears to shed.

As they stumble across the fairgrounds,

Zuzanna reflects privately that it's lucky that Elspeth was the automaton who gained sentience. In the Fair's clean-swept streets, where electric streetlamps pierce the gloom and make the enormous white buildings glow, her skin looks close enough to human, and the unnatural brightness of her eyes is barely noticeable. She is dressed in the latest fashion, a white blouse and black skirt, an auburn-haired Gibson girl, with her long neck covered by a high collar. This is most fortunate, as her metal-skinned sisters were clad in costumes of historical figures: Joan of Arc, Cleopatra, Mary Magdalene, any of which would have been far more conspicuous as she made her way across the fairgrounds, especially with shining metal skin.

The two women, one ordinary and one surreally beautiful, walk arm-in-arm like close friends, though their true intent is to make Elspeth's halting, awkward gait less noticeable. Pressed so close together Zuzanna can smell the oil used to lubricate the automaton's joints. The metal limbs click and groan with each motion, a painful sound that makes Zuzanna wince.

Zuzanna waves absently to a security

guard as they hurry across one of the scenic bridges over the elegant canals that traverse the park. "This is truly lovely," Elspeth observes, but the words sound unconvincing in her tinny, emotionless monotone.

The shanty is a well-known structure on the outskirts of the fairgrounds. It has been a gathering place for the Fair's many architects, engineers and designers since the Fair was little more than an improbable dream, and Zuzanna can only hope that Professor Campion will be among the men who gather there. The hour is late, and many of the men will have already gone home, she thinks, but as they round the last corner and spy the little cottage, hope swells in her breast. The windows are ablaze with light, smoke pours from the chimney, and brusque male laughter drifts through the night air to meet the women approaching the house.

Zuzanna and the automaton stand before the door for a few moments while Zuzanna tries to work up the courage to knock. Finally it is Elspeth who boldly lifts the knocker and slams it back down three times in quick succession.

"Entree!" A chorus of male voices calls,

and there is more baritone laughter.

Elspeth pushes the door open and ushers Zuzanna ahead of her.

Stunned silence greets her entry. A dozen pairs of curious eyes turn to look at the new arrival. The room is thick with cigar smoke and Zuzanna cannot stop herself from coughing. The men quickly stub out their cigars and fan at the air; some look apologetic, as if a woman's presence has made them realize their own boorish behavior, and others look vaguely hostile at the interruption.

"What can we do for you, my dear?" A tall man asks gruffly, stepping forward to greet her.

"I'm so terribly, terribly sorry to bother you," Zuzanna says in her most apologetic tone, "I'm Zuzanna Uritiski; I work in the Electricity Building. I need Professor Campion, right away."

"Is there a fire?" Someone asks, and several people gasp.

"No, no fire. But something urgent. There's a problem with one of his automatons."

"Oh, haha, we took bets on when they'd start having trouble! Anyone have three months then?"

"Is he here? Professor Campion, I mean?" Zuzanna asks over the laughter.

"Yes, I'm here, I'm here," says Professor Campion, emerging from a doorway.

The Professor is an ordinary man in nearly every respect. He is average height, with an appropriately fashionable moustache, and wears a brown suit and leather shoes that desperately need polishing. His only truly standout feature, the one that sets him apart from all the other men present, are his shrewd, kind eyes. They are cobalt blue, a shade that Zuzanna has seen in her dreams ever since her first encounter with the man.

"What seems to be the problem?" The Professor asks when Zuzanna remains speechless. He is standing so close, and his eyes are fixed so intently upon her face, that she cannot find any words to explain.

"You'll have to come with me," she finally stutters, blushing furiously.

The Professor frowns, tugs at his moustache, and then collects his bowler from the hat stand near the door. He follows Zuzanna out into the balmy summer night, shutting the door behind him.

"Now tell me the meaning of this," the Professor says in an urgent whisper.

Before Zuzanna can reply, Elspeth steps out from the darkness into the pool of light cast by the nearest streetlamp. Her pale skin and red hair sparkle as if they contain motes of gold dust, and she is so lovely that both Zuzanna and Professor Campion catch their breaths.

After a few moments of shocked silence, the Professor turns to Zuzanna. "What have you done?!" he hisses, grasping her roughly by the elbow and dragging her away from the shanty, toward the automaton.

"Me?!" Zuzanna cries, utterly confused. She is too shocked to pull away, instead allowing herself to be dragged.

"How did you get poor Elspeth out here, in the elements? And why would you do such a thing? The exhibit will be doomed if anything happens to her! Do you have any idea of her value?!"

"Professor Campion, I presume?" Elspeth says, taking another step toward them.

The Professor draws up short, so surprised by the automaton's words that he releases Zuzanna, who backs away from him. Professor Campion is only a few feet from his creation now; at last he can see the intelligence in her face, the awkwardness of her limbs, the way her eyes follow his movements. "Pardon?" he says, shaking his head as if to clear it of cobwebs.

"I imagine you are quite shocked to find that your mechanical creation has a soul," Elspeth says, her voice ringing in the quiet of the dark fairgrounds. "I assure you that you are no more shocked than I. And this is why I must ask you several very important questions about this automaton."

Professor Campion is just staring at her now, his jaw hanging slack, his hands limp at his sides. Zuzanna approaches him cautiously, one hand covering the painful bruise where he gripped her elbow.

"You're not mad," Zuzanna tells him, watching his face closely, slightly afraid that he might grab her again.

His eyes swivel from the automaton to Zuzanna, then back to Elspeth again. His mouth works a few times, as if he would speak, but has forgotten how to form words Then tears fill his eyes and he stammers softly, nearly inaudibly. "Betsy? Have you come back to me?"

"Betsy? No.," Elspeth says impatiently. "I understand you are confused, but I simply do not have time for this. I have a mission to complete, and I must determine how much time I have remaining in this body. Can you tell me how long a human soul can inhabit a mechanical form such as this?"

The Professor shakes his head again, this time more fervently, and then clears his throat. Then, in a tone that betrays no surprise or bewilderment, he says simply, "We must talk somewhere in private. I suggest that you accompany me to my hotel. It's only a few blocks away."

He starts to turn, but Zuzanna catches at his sleeve. "You'll have to help me support Elspeth. She's still feeling out how to use her legs."

Professor Campion's eyes widen, but then he returns to his façade of normalcy, nodding curtly and positioning himself with one elbow

extended so that Elspeth might lean on him.
Zuzanna takes up the other side, and the three of
them begin a slow, halting, awkward stroll across
the remainder of the park and out into the City,
for all the world looking like a trio of old friends
visiting the Fair and wandering drunkenly back
to their hotel.

The Hyde Park Hotel is a huge, elegant
building, constructed for the Fair and housing
many of its most prestigious guests and investors.
While most visitors are awed by the classical
architecture and gold-leafed frescoes, Zuzanna
immediately thinks of how difficult it must be to
keep the vaulted rafters free of dust. She lowers
her head upon their entrance, hoping to hide
her face somewhat as she makes her way into the
elevator with Professor Campion and Elspeth.
Her cheeks are burning with what she perceives
to be the curious eyes of the night porters and
bellmen, watching the Professor ascend to his
suite with two young women, the three of them
pressed together with appalling familiarity. She is
terrified that her reputation will be ruined.

As the Professor pours drinks—he
has only bourbon, and pours only for himself

and Zuzanna—she begins wringing her hands anxiously. Distracted by the more pressing matter of the automaton, Professor Campion leaves her bourbon on the table rather than handing it to her as a good host ought to under ordinary circumstances. Zuzanna can hardly blame him for being forgetful of propriety; Elspeth's presence is utterly consuming for them both.

"I am what you might consider to be a wandering spirit," Elspeth says without preamble. Her voice is loud in the silent room, without open air to disperse the volume or the noise of the bustling City that, even late at night, muffles conversation. "I came to possess this body after my last one was rendered unusable. I am able to possess only living forms, Professor Campion, and thus you perceive my dilemma. Can you advise me as to how I came to inhabit this form if it is truly mechanical? And, more importantly, can you tell me how long I might expect to remain in possession of it?"

Professor Campion places his glass on the table and puts his hands in his pockets. He presses his lips into a thin line as he considers his words. Then he sighs and says, "What I'm about to reveal cannot leave this room."

His eyes are focused on Zuzanna, who frowns. "I can keep your confidence," she says, a little defensively.

"You must understand that what I have done is at best amoral and at worst illegal. I do not reveal it lightly." He moves to the settee upon which Elspeth sits, and when he speaks, he addresses the automaton. "The original exhibit for the Fair was not of my design. It was primarily designed by my wife, Elisabeth— Betsy—who sadly died a few months ago, before the automatons were complete." He says the words without inflection, and in a rapid, staccato delivery, as if he cannot stop to place emphasis on words, or else he will regret them or hesitate to divulge some important detail. "Betsy was brilliant, a student of the British Royal Institute. When she died, I elected to carry on the project without her, so that her vision would be made reality. I did it to honor her."

He hesitates, and Zuzanna, thinking that she knows where the story is going, says softly, "What did you do?"

Professor Campion still refuses to

look at Zuzanna. "I loved my wife so much, I couldn't bear the thought of her passing. All that brilliance stolen from the world . . . I wanted to preserve her. It was madness, but I wanted to keep what I could . . . and so I prepared one of the automatons to be her new body. Upon the moment of her death I removed what organs I could save and implanted them in a new, mechanical shell."

Zuzanna gasps, the truth being worse than even the story her furtive imagination has concocted.

Professor Campion reaches into his jacket pocket and removes a tiny screwdriver. Without asking permission or announcing his intentions, he begins unbuttoning Elspeth's blouse while holding the screwdriver between his teeth. His hands are surprisingly delicate and feminine, his long, tapered fingers crisscrossed with scars both fresh and well-healed. Elspeth makes no protest as he peels back the edges of the blouse, revealing the expanse of her metal chest, and then uses the screwdriver to carefully remove several screws. He places each tiny screw on the tray beside his glass of bourbon. His movements are precise and practiced, his hands careful and deliberate.

Finally, the last screw plinking into the tray, the Professor opens a hinged door on Elspeth's chest. Inside, in the recesses of her metal body, several organs—a heart? lungs?—pulse and undulate wetly. Zuzanna has never seen internal human organs before, and the sight is truly disturbing. She has to turn away for fear that she might vomit.

"I chose the Electricity Building for the automatons because they use so much power," Professor Campion says softly in the guilt-laden quiet. "Elspeth requires more power than the others combined to keep her heart beating. But the organs won't survive forever, even with an endless source of power. I was planning to let her go once the Fair was ended."

Abruptly, Elspeth snaps shut the gate on her chest. "Very well. How long can I survive away from the Electricity Building?"

"That's just it," Professor Campion says, and his voice is bleak now. "You shouldn't be able to survive without a constant source of power at all. I don't know how you even left the building. You must have unplugged your wiring when you left the stage." He shakes his head and stares at her with undisguised wonder. "This shouldn't even be possible."

Elspeth is speechless for a moment, and then says, "Then I must act quickly. My normal methods will not do. No one can guarantee that I will be able to move on from this automaton even if the organs fail. I might be trapped in this body forever, even as it becomes a useless lump of steel and circuits. The final battle must be fought, and this vessel will be the valiant steed upon which I make my last desperate joust." She looks pointedly at the Professor. "Please replace the screws."

Professor Campion obeys, but his hands are shaking now, so replacing each screw takes considerably longer than did removal.

"What is your mission then?" Zuzanna finally asks. She has drunk two fingerfuls of bourbon and her head is feeling a little flimsy.

"It is perhaps better that you do not know."

Zuzanna chortles, an unladylike sound. "Do you really think you can accomplish anything on your own? You can barely walk."

"The burden is mine to bear, not yours. I have pursued this mission for a dozen lifetimes and I have always worked alone."

"And how did that work out for you?" Zuzanna demands, swinging her arm so that a little bourbon splashes out of her glass. "It seems to me that if you'd asked for help sooner maybe you could have completed your mission before now."

"I have suffered lifetimes of misery," Elspeth says. "In the pursuit of this mission, I have seen horrors that cannot be unseen, suffered tortures of all kinds, and felt the kind of fear and madness that drives men to suicide."

"And you have never once sought help?" The Professor says without looking up from his task. "How many people were made to suffer because your pride insisted that you must complete the mission alone?"

Though the Professor's words are nonchalantly delivered, they cause Elspeth to pause. She considers this, blinking slowly. Then her cold gaze settles on Zuzanna. "You must understand that if you help me, you endanger your very lives."

"We understand. Let us decide whether we want to help you," Zuzanna says.

Elspeth nods once, succinctly. "I am in pursuit of what you would call a demon: an inhuman force of evil."

Now Professor Campion chortles incredulously. "A demon?"

"You are having a conversation with an automaton possessed by a soul from another plane and yet you doubt the existence of demons?" Elspeth asks.

The Professor shifts uncomfortably, then shrugs and says, "You have a point."

"This demon has lead me on a pursuit across the globe for the last several centuries. He possesses those who already have immoral tendencies, those who can already murder and maim without conscience, and drives them to new heights of madness. His favorite victims are women and children, and he prefers to make them love and trust him before he destroys them. Sometimes he grows frustrated and kills wantonly, recklessly, which allows me to track him. In England he took to killing prostitutes in gruesome ways—"

"Wait," Zuzanna says, putting down her glass, "you're chasing Jack the Ripper?!"

Elspeth nods. "Just so. But the demon abandoned that body when I caught him. The man who committed those murders is dead; I killed him myself. But the creature who inhabited the body kills on."

"And he's here? In Chicago?"

"Yes. Part of the spell that allows me to remain earth-bound after death allows me to reincarnate near him. When inhabiting a human host, I can see the demon's true form beneath the human facade; he cannot hide from me." Elspeth pauses, considering how many details she should divulge, then continues. "His current host is a man named Holmes. Henry H. Holmes."

Zuzanna gasps and covers her mouth. "I applied to work in his drugstore," she groans. "I met him, and thought him quite charming. I was devastated when he didn't hire me."

"Consider yourself lucky that you are not his type," Elspeth replies, buttoning her blouse with stiff fingers. "He prefers slender blond women, ones with tractable personalities. He has for four hundred years."

"Why can't you just call the police?" Professor Campion asks, leaning over to assist the automaton with her difficult buttons. "If he's truly murdering women there's bound to be evidence, and they can lock him up."

"He will only do as he has done a dozen times or more: abandon the body and go in search of a new vessel, free to kill again. He must be bound to the body before I can do him harm, so that man and demon become one entity. There is a ritual that will perform that task, though I have never successfully completed it before . . . perhaps because the rite is meant to be performed by a woman."

Both of them turn to look at Zuzanna. She is staring fixedly at some point on the wall, her brown eyes huge and glistening, her hands still covering her mouth as if in shock.

Professor Campion rises from the settee and moves to the divan. His dark blue eyes are full of concern and sympathy, and he takes Zuzanna's hands between his in a way that would ordinarily be far too familiar for the troubled young woman; but at the moment, all she can think about are Holmes's eyes, which she remembers distinctly. They were also blue, but a cold, clear, icy blue. She shivers as if caught in a sudden draught.

"If you are too fearful to help me, you may quit now. No one will blame you," Elspeth says without inflection, struggling with the last few buttons.

"Are you sure he's the killer?" Zuzanna asks breathily. "How can you know that the demon has possessed him?"

Elspeth's fingers grow still against her chest. "I have seen him kill. You do not want to know more than that. You must trust me."

"Trust you? We don't even know you! You could be the demon, in the end, trying to convince us to kill an innocent man!" Zuzanna cries. She is shaking uncontrollably now, her voice growing hysterical.

Professor Campion puts his arm around the distraught woman's shoulders and pulls her close to him. "Have you seen Elspeth hurt anyone? Has she done anything to lead you to believe that she is evil?"

Calming a little, Zuzanna begins to realize the compromising position in which she finds herself and pushes away from the Professor. "You don't understand, Professor. Mr. Holmes was so kind and so genuine. I don't see how he could be evil. I need proof, and you should as well."

They both look at Elspeth, who has given up on the blouse buttons and is sitting dejectedly. She regards them both with blank glass eyes, then sighs softly and says, "I can provide you with proof, but you will regret asking to see it." When both of them refuse to give ground, she says, "Professor, you will have to find us a priest while we fashion the spell."

While the Professor goes in search for a man of the cloth, Zuzanna and Elspeth make themselves comfortable and set about writing a spell. Elspeth has the spell memorized, but it is in her native language. The best recitation, she tells Zuzanna, would be from memory, but the words must be in Elspeth's native tongue; there's no way Zuzanna can memorize the strange sounds in only a few hours. Instead, hotel stationery and a fountain pen are ordered from the front desk, along with a pot of strong, black coffee to keep Zuzanna awake. The maid sits at the writing desk, taking Elspeth's dictation. She writes each alien sound phonetically, practices pronouncing it, and then moves on to the next phrase. The work is painstaking and her fingers are cramped and ink-stained by the time the Professor returns, hours later, with a small, balding Irish priest from St. James Cathedral in tow.

The priest looks confused upon seeing the finely appointed suite. "I had to tell him my mother was dying and needed last rites," Professor Campion says apologetically, shrugging.

"You did as you needed to do," Elspeth says from the settee, where she has remained fixed as a rooted tree all night. "Welcome, Father. Did you bring the anointing oil?"

"I, uh, yes, but why?" The priest asks, his eyebrows drawn together in bafflement.

"I need you to anoint this woman and bless her against evil."

"I don't understand."

"It's really very simple. Use the oil, anoint her brow, give her a simple blessing, and then you may be on your way."

The priest hesitates, so Zuzanna rises from the desk, walks over to the priest, and kneels before him, smiling. "We are very religious people," she tells him.

Finally the man uncorks the bottle of anointing oil, muttering under his breath, and performs a perfunctory blessing. The oil, as he describes the shape of a cross on her forehead, is slick and surprisingly warm. When he replaces the cork in the bottle Zuzanna is disappointed to find that she feels no different, no stronger, no more proofed against wickedness.

Professor Campion gives the priest a donation and sends the man home.

"How goes the spell?" he asks, pouring himself the last dregs of coffee.

"As well as we could hope, given our restrictions of time and language. Now that we have the priest's blessing I think we should not wait."

Zuzanna is startled. "You want to go now?"

"Yes. There's no sense in putting off the inevitable, and I do not know when this body will become useless. Gather your pages and let's go."

Less than an hour later, Zuzanna waits

on the small doorstep at the kitchen door of the World's Fair Hotel a massive structure that looms across six full city blocks, a mammoth building that is as ominous as an ancient castle. She fights the urge to scratch at her forehead, where she imagines she can still feel the priest's fingers lingering on her skin. She is intensely aware that she is alone, though she knows that Elspeth and Professor Campion wait only a dozen feet away, just around the corner. In the wee hours, after a few cups of coffee and a rousing speech from Elspeth about the nature of evil, Zuzanna had been eager to volunteer for this duty. But now as dawn approaches she is exhausted, feeling very small and vulnerable looking up at the demon's enormous castle, and she wonders why she insisted so stridently on proof of evil.

The door opens and, to her surprise, it is Holmes who greets her. His face is haggard, his chin unshaven, and he wears a housecoat and room shoes. He looks pleasantly surprised to see her standing on his stoop, alone and unprotected, one small suitcase held before her like a talisman.

"I'm so sorry, did I wake you?" She asks, genuinely contrite.

Though he has met her before, conversed with her for an hour over tea while he charmed her thoroughly, Holmes's face shows no hint of recognition. "No, don't worry. I have been up all night working on a difficult case. I'm a doctor." He smiles the winsome grin that made her heart race on their first meeting; now, knowing that he may well have been using this easy charm to lure women to their gruesome deaths, Zuzanna finds the smile repulsive.

The cross on her brow itches.

"Do you have any rooms?" Zuzanna asks, following the script agreed upon with her cohorts. Elspeth had warned her that he would likely not remember her, for women are little more than interchangeable pegs in his mind; she mustn't call his attention to this, lest she rouse his suspicion.

The itching becomes more intense, increasingly like burning.

Holmes opens his mouth to answer her, his smile still intact, but the cross flares, a bright light on Zuzanna's brow. She cries out in pain, her hand going to her forehead to scratch at the oil smear. Holmes lets out an inhuman scream that raises the hairs on her arms, his face contorting horribly into something unnatural, and slams the door. She can hear the bolts sliding home as he locks her out.

Zuzanna turns and runs across the street and around the corner, where she slams into Elspeth and Professor Campion, who folds his arms around her immediately.

"Are you satisfied?" Elspeth asks, and it is obvious that she would smirk if her face were capable of producing more than one expression.

Zuzanna nods, scratching at her forehead. "It was horrible."

"You're trembling," Professor Campion says, holding her against his chest and making no movement to release her from his embrace. She does not push him away.

After the tumultuous hours of the previous evening she is more exhausted than she has ever been in her life, and propriety is the least of her concerns.

While the humans huddle together, Elspeth stands alone, seemingly impervious to fear. She gazes steadfastly at the World's Fair Hotel, eyeing it the way a Hun must have eyed the Great Wall.

The street is becoming busy as dawn approaches. Bakers and shopkeepers bustle past on their way to their shops, and newsboys run to the printer for the day's first edition.

Zuzanna misses the wide, clean avenues of the Fair. The streets of Chicago proper are dark and narrow and smell like a sewer.

"We must go in now, before he takes precautions," the automaton says. "If you wish to back out, I will not think less of you. Having met him, and seen a small part of his true self, you are no doubt terrified, and I cannot blame you for that. It will only be worse from here."

"Why aren't you afraid?" Zuzanna asks, leaning into the Professor's arms.

"I have nothing to lose."

Elspeth's words are met with heavy silence.

"If you want to stay here, we can go on without you," Professor Campion tells Zuzanna.

"If you're going in, I'm going in," Zuzanna replies stubbornly.

"Then that's settled," Elspeth says before they can discuss it further. "Professor, keep your hand on your pistol. Miss Utriski, do you have the pages?"

Zuzanna opens the small suitcase borrowed from Professor Campion's suite. She pulls out the sheaf of papers inscribed with the binding spell and clutches them to her chest. She leaves the suitcase on the sidewalk; whether it will be there when they return seems of little concern at the moment. "I'm ready," she tells the automaton.

"Remember the plan. And no matter what the demon tells you, do not deviate. He will lie, cajole, threaten and tempt you if it will do him good. If you fail in your part, we will all be doomed."

Zuzanna and Professor Campion both nod soberly and together the trio walks to the front entrance of the hotel. Time seems to slow for Zuzanna during this stroll, as she and the Professor assist Elspeth, whose flailing limbs are becoming increasingly difficult to control. Every step seems to have heavy significance, every moment singing as if it might be her last.

The small man who answers the door of the World's Fair Hotel reminds Zuzanna of a rat.

He introduces himself as Mr. Pitezel and invites them all inside without a hint of suspicion. His black eyes gleam as he observes the women. One of his hands brushes Zuzanna's and she stiffens, moving closer to Professor Campion reflexively. Pitezel bows apologetically, but his moustache twitches, giving away his annoyance. He has not half the charm and debonair ease of Holmes.

As soon as the door closes Professor Campion draws the pistol and points it at Pitezel. "Upstairs," he says, his voice as low and menacing as he can make it.

Pitezel sucks in his breath with a hiss. "The safe is in Mr. Holmes's office, but I don't have the key," he says, mistaking them for burglars.

"Upstairs," Professor Campion repeats.

After a moment of hesitation, Pitezel turns and heads for the stairs. Professor Campion follows him closely.

Elspeth and Zuzanna wait, Elspeth unable to traverse the stairs easily and Zuzanna unwilling to leave her alone, while the Professor locks the man in the nearest guest room. The huge grandfather clock in the foyer chimes forebodingly. Long moments seem to stretch endlessly, and Zuzanna again wonders whether she will meet her death in this house.

When at last the Professor returns, Elspeth leads them unerringly to the basement door. Zuzanna wonders for the first time how their leader knows the layout of the hotel so intimately. It occurs to her that perhaps Elspeth's knowledge of Holmes's proclivities is truly first-hand, and she has to fight back tears at this horrifying thought.

Elspeth gives them one last chance to quit the plan before they descend. "What you see here will be with you forever," she explains. But her companions persist, so they open the door and begin the descent into what Zuzanna will later recall as the bowels of Hell.

Descending is difficult for Elspeth and takes her some time. Finally, they reach the bottom of the stairs and cluster before another door. Elspeth nods to Professor Campion, who holds his pistol skyward with one hand and turns the knob with the other.

The smell hits them before the sights: decay, death, and chemicals. Zuzanna covers her nose and mouth with a handkerchief; the scent of Chicago's noisome streets is delightful by comparison. Professor Campion turns vaguely green. Elspeth forges ahead, unperturbed, her lack of olfactory senses a benefit.

The room beyond the door is outfitted like a combined butcher shop and morgue. Huge hooks dangle from the ceiling, and the walls are outfitted with various implements--hatchets, bone saws, stilettos. The floor is metal and a drain has been installed in the center. Above the drain there is a dissecting table. The ceiling above the table is decorated with strange sigils, glyphs of some alien alphabet, carelessly inscribed in what looks at first like brown paint, but which Zuzanna gradually realizes must be blood.

The table is inhabited by a cadaver, its chest flayed, skin removed from its face, so that its sex is indeterminate from this angle. The body is so fresh that the revealed innards still gleam wetly; Zuzanna catches glimpses of red muscle and white bone before she has to look away. At the end of the table, still attached to the corpse's head, a long fall of golden hair trails from the table to the floor.

It is this last observation that drives Zuzanna into a fit of retching.

Behind the cadaver, on the other side of the table, Holmes sits with his arms coated in blood. He holds a scalpel in his hand, as if he is performing some delicate surgery, and he looks up at them in surprise and confusion. He regards Zuzanna, bent at the waist to vomit beside the door, with bafflement, then recognition, and at last with anger.

His cold blue eyes, gray in the colorless electric lights, flick from Zuzanna to Professor Campion, whose pistol is pointed firmly at Holmes's head, and then to Elspeth, who is trying to creep around the dissection table. She is failing utterly, her jerky steps making her conspicuous. Holmes's apparent confusion allows her to get closer to him than she would have otherwise, however, and with one last burst of energy, she lurches forward, one arm thrust out, and clamps her fingers down on Holmes's bloody arm.

Holmes stares at the strange hand on his wrist and lets out a bark of laughter. "What is this?" he asks. He looks up at Elspeth's face, and there is recognition there. "My old nemesis.

You've changed the game at last, then? But . . ."
He shakes his head, unable to quite understand
what is wrong.

Elspeth looks to Zuzanna. "Read the
words!" she shouts over Holmes's confused
mutterings.

Zuzanna's mouth tastes like bile, but it
makes the smell of death and chloroform easier
to ignore. She tries to read the pages clutched in
her hands, but she finds that her vision is blurred
and her arms shaking, making it impossible to
see the phrases. She dashes the tears from her eyes
and holds the pages up high enough that they
cover the gruesome sight on the dissection table,
hoping that if she blocks the cadaver from view
perhaps her trembling will ease.

Suddenly Professor Campion is at her
side. He keeps the pistol trained on Holmes as he
reaches with his other hand to steady Zuzanna's
elbow. The trembling gradually fades, the tide
of tears bulwarked by the Professor's presence,
enough that she can eventually see the letters
marked on the page.

Hesitantly at first, with halting stops
and starts, Zuzanna begins to read. She cannot

be sure that she is reading the alien phrases correctly, but she persists, gaining confidence with Professor Campion's hand steadying her. Gradually, her voice grows louder and more sure, the phrases taking on a cadence, the sounds gaining speed and rhythm. Soon she is reading as if the language were her own, as if the sounds have meaning to her, and they seem to pour from her mouth effortlessly. A page drops to the floor as she finishes it.

Now the words seem to crackle as they leave her lips, and the air before her begins to shimmer in response to the magic. The electric lights flicker and dim, and the cross on her forehead glows bright white, a star to illuminate the darkness.

Holmes lets out an unearthly howl. Heedless of the pistol he still clutches in his right hand, Professor Campion covers his ears to block out the sound. Zuzanna is miraculously unfazed and continues reading; momentarily she lets a second page drop to the floor.

The demon, realizing the meaning behind the sounds as the air in the room becomes hot and dense, tries to wriggle free of Elspeth's unnaturally strong grip, but finds that her fingers are like a vise. He gropes for the tray, snatching up a scalpel, and stabs the instrument into her hand; when she fails to react he grabs for more tools and tries again. Each attempt to do violence to the automaton is met with the same implacable, glassy stare and blank smile. He bellows his frustration and curses at her in the language of their native world, invectives he probably has not used in hundreds of years.

Finally, the last page reached and his panic complete, Holmes is apparently desperate, his undoing nearly upon him. He yanks hard on his right arm, trying to either pull it free of Elspeth's grip or pull himself free of the arm. He screams as tendons pop and flesh tears, dislocating his humerus from the shoulder socket. Then, to his surprise, his arm comes completely free of the automaton's grasp all at once, and he stumbles away from her.

Both Holmes and Elspeth stare in shock at the glove of flesh that has come free from her hand, flopping ineffectually to the floor. The automaton regards her unsheathed metal fingers, her mouth agape, uttering a soft, tinny whimper.

Holmes loses no time; he launches himself in one, impossible leap over the cadaver—upsetting the dissection table and spilling both corpse and dissection tools onto the floor—at the woman still reading the spell that will doom him if he allows her to complete it.

Professor Campion cries out wordlessly, and though he was instructed not to fire the pistol until the spell is complete, he pulls the trigger.

Gunfire in such an enclosed space is deafening. Both Zuzanna and Professor Campion crumple to the floor, clapping their palms over their ears in a vain attempt to block the painful ringing sound. They both writhe on the floor screaming.

After a few moments of searing pain, the echoes of the gunshot fade a little, and Zuzanna sits up, removing her hands from her ears. Sprawled only inches from her on the metal floor is Holmes, most of his face blasted away by the close-range pistol shot, his blood oozing across the floor to the drain.

Elspeth is crouched beside him, her metal fingers lifting his head, hopeful that perhaps he is still alive. Zuzanna tries to ask if the demon is dead, but she cannot even hear her own words over the constant ringing sound. Elspeth simply looks up, her green eyes huge and doll-like, and shakes her head definitively.

Professor Campion rises and helps Zuzanna to her feet. When he speaks, his voice sounds muffled and small, tinny as the automaton's own. "Let's burn this place to the ground," he says, and his expression is hard and triumphant.

Elspeth

Fire is a great equalizer: It ravages the palatial estates of the wealthy just as it razes the homes of the poor. The demon's murder castle, constructed over years of careful plotting and scheming, is no exception, and there is admittedly some satisfaction in watching the destruction of something so grand and so evil, knowing that its rooms will never again be used for torture.

My companions' faces, lit by the golden-orange glow of the massive blaze, are triumphant and relieved. They believe that we have done the world some great good, and now there will be a time of rest and rejuvenation before the demon rises again. I don't tell them that by failing to destroy the creature, we may have doomed them both to a fate more miserable than death. The demon knows their faces now; worse, his minion knows us, and he yet lives, released because we could not bring ourselves to commit cold-blooded murder. Both demon and servant will stop at nothing to destroy us utterly.

Unless we can find the creature and make another attempt to bind and truly eradicate him, he will hunt us down and consume everyone we love as completely as the fire consumes his hotel. He will be relentless. I fear for these poor people, these volunteers whom I regret recruiting, who think the war is over with the kind of hopeful naïveté that has no place in the struggle against evil.

I do not tell them that the battle has only just begun; there will be time for that later. For now, I let them have their small triumph, and we watch the castle burn.

PART 2

Archie

At first glance, the tableau is familiar: a man, shirtsleeves rolled up and affixed with garters, leans over a figure on a table, tools in hand, conducting some delicate surgery. His assistant, a woman in a black dress, leans over and blots at his perspiring forehead with a white cotton handkerchief. The room is utterly silent except for the surgeon's labored breathing and the muffled sounds of motorcars and carriages passing in the busy streets below the window.

But the scene is not entirely what it seems.

When the surgeon leans back, the patient on the table becomes visible. She is an extraordinarily beautiful woman, with skin smooth as a newborn babe's and huge emerald eyes. Her hair is the same shade of scarlet viewed when the sun sets over the ocean, lighting the sky with shimmering brilliance. She is captivating.

"Perhaps we should take a respite,"

the patient suggests. Her voice is a startling monotone, tinny and strange.

The surgeon sighs. "I've almost got it," he says.

"You've been doing this for three hours, Archie. I think it's time for a cup of tea. Your hands aren't getting any steadier," his assistant says. Her voice is simultaneously gentle and stern.

Archie throws the tools into the tray beside the table. "I almost had it."

When he moves away from the bench, the object of his intense labor becomes fully visible: the patient's right arm, devoid of flesh, revealing a metal skeleton held together with wire and screws.

The patient sits up. "I think perhaps this arm is beyond help now, Professor."

"No. You should be more durable than that."

"Elspeth's body wasn't made for this kind of wear," the assistant says as she helps the mechanical woman swing her legs over the edge of the table. Slowly, she lowers the patient into a wheelchair, covering her legs with a plaid blanket. "She was made for singing at the Columbian

World's Fair, not for doing battle with demons."

Elspeth regards her creator with glassy eyes that betray no emotion. "You have done your best, Professor, and you are to be commended for it, but unfortunately the deterioration of this body is happening more quickly than expected. There may be no reversal."

"I only wish I could build you a replacement," Archie says. "Or we could cannibalize one of the other automatons at the Fair. But the Fair Committee is already after my head . . . " His musings taper off into a weary sigh.

"It would only postpone the inevitable. My gran always said you do the best with what you're given," the assistant volunteers, trying to sound cheerful, but when she smiles her dark eyes still hold a deep sadness.

"Ah, Zuzanna, always trying to find the light in the darkness," Archie replies, and his smile is full of genuine warmth and affection.

As if oblivious to the chemistry passing between her companions, the automaton uses her good arm to wheel herself across the room to the window. "We must do the ritual tonight," she says, gazing out at the dusty streets of Chicago.

"Tonight?" Zuzanna repeats, her voice high with distress. "How can we? You can barely move!"

"And thus the urgency. Who knows when this body will fail completely? We need to make this happen now, before I become entirely useless."

The three companions are quiet for a few moments, each considering the import of the automaton's proclamation.

"It makes sense," Archie says, shrugging his broad shoulders. "But that doesn't mean we have to like it."

"Miss Uritski will have to obtain the last remaining item on the list," Elspeth says.

Zuzanna draws a slip of paper from her apron pocket. "I can go to the butcher shop down the road. It won't take but a moment." She unties her apron and drapes it over the back of the wide divan that dominates the parlor of the suite. She pulls a pair of gloves over her dainty hands, covers her dark coif with a wide-brimmed hat, and quietly leaves.

She doesn't ask whether either of her

companions want to accompany her.

When the door closes behind his assistant, Archie lets out a deep, soulful sigh.

"You should rest. We have a long night ahead of us," Elspeth tells him from her place near the window.

Archie goes to the bar instead, pouring himself a half glass of bourbon. He swirls the amber liquid in the glass and then drinks it down in two big gulps. "I don't want her to do it," he says, his courage bolstered by the alcohol.

"We have no other choice."

"It's dangerous. She slept for three straight days after the last time." He shudders, remembering vividly the night, three months ago in the Fall of 1893, when he and Elspeth and Zuzanna had tried to take down the demon, the night Zuzanna had performed magic for the first time . . . and had nearly died from the aftereffects. He can still smell the abattoir stench of the demon's vivisection room.

"I recognize that there is some personal risk, for her especially. But the decision must be hers."

"She'd sell you her skin if she thought

it would save a stranger's soul! You're taking advantage."

"Miss Uritski is an adult possessed of all her mental faculties. Her decisions should be her own."

"There has to be another way."

"The spell must be performed by a woman!" Elspeth's words are emphasized by a well-timed involuntary spasm of her right arm, her wrist knocking against the windowsill. She reaches with her left hand to grasp her right wrist, bringing the recalcitrant hand to rest in her lap. "You saw the depth of her power, Professor Campion. She was made for this; it is her destiny."

"Destiny! Pah!" Archie pours himself more bourbon. "No such beast. It's your destiny we're fulfilling here, your mission."

"And what would you have me do, Professor?" Elspeth replies, her head turning on her neck to regard him at an awkward, ugly angle, reminding him of her inhumanity. "I cannot involve another woman, but neither can I perform the ritual myself. If we fail to find the demon, both you and Miss Uritski are doomed.

I regret having involved you, but there is no retreat. We must see this through, or your lives are forfeit."

"The demon is dead. We haven't heard a thing from him or that ratty Pietzel man in months. This whole thing is unnecessary." Archie is enjoying the floating feeling that results from drinking his bourbon without food. Of late, he knows he's been drinking more than he should, but finds that he doesn't care. Ever since that night in the World's Fair Hotel, his bourbon glass has rarely been empty. He requires half a bottle before bed each night to obliterate the nightmares that haunt his sleep.

"The demon is not dead, and Pietzel yet continues to serve him. He only lays low in the hopes of evading us until he can grow strong enough to do battle. Somewhere, likely within Chicago itself, they scheme against us."

Archie doesn't respond; he stares at the bourbon swirling in his glass as if hypnotized. The room is quiet for a few moments, the hubbub outside the hotel a forgettable roar, a clock on the mantle softly ticking away the minutes. Archie regrets failing to kill the demon's assistant, the rat-like Pietzel, and his chest feels tight with this raging internal conflict. What kind of man regrets being merciful? He is paralyzed by indecision and regret.

The pensive quiet is suddenly broken by a great crashing sound, and Archie goes to the window to investigate. Three stories down, a motorcar has met with a lamppost. A woman's motionless body is sprawled in the street, clad all in black, rapidly surrounded by concerned onlookers. Archie's heart leaps into his throat. With so much dust and so many people, he can't discern the identity of the woman in the street. Is it Zuzanna?

Finally someone helps the woman to her feet; her hat slips back and reveals a head of bright white hair and a face that is old enough to be Zuzanna's mother. Archie releases the breath he'd been holding.

"You should really tell her," Elspeth says, her voice sharp as a knife.

"Tell her what?" Archie asks absently, still observing the scene below the window.

"Tell her how you feel."

Archie turns from the window to regard

the automaton. Bathed in the dusky sunlight, filtered by Chicago's pollution and the thick window glass, she is utterly beautiful, the hazy light giving her a surreal quality, as if she has just stepped out of a painting.

A painting of Archie's late wife.

"How can I while the face of my dead Betsy looks on?" he asks, the words tumbling from his lips before he can stop them.

Elspeth can't cry, or frown, or even draw her eyebrows together in concern, but she leans back in her wheelchair and looks away from him. The gesture is enough to communicate her sadness.

"I'm sorry," Archie says immediately. "I think I've had too much bourbon."

"I should say so," Elspeth agrees.

"You know, I didn't really love Betsy." Talking about his late wife allows Archie to think about something other than Pietzel, the escaped demon, and the horrors of the demon's basement lair.

Elspeth looks up, intrigued, green eyes glittering.

"She married me to give her research

credibility in scientific circles; I married her to give my name credibility in social circles. We were just colleagues, married for convenience. We didn't love each other—not at first, anyway."

Elspeth doesn't speak.

"But she was so brilliant. Ultimately that's what won me over, you know. How could I not love her mind? And then I thought what a pity it would be not to pass on that brilliance." Archie's pupils dilate; he stops speaking as he becomes lost in reverie, a distant memory of the woman he once called his wife. In trying not to concentrate on the traumatic events of three months before, Archie has opened another gaping wound from the past, one that he thought was healed, but which now aches with renewed vigor.

Elspeth opens her mouth to speak, but just at that moment the door of the suite opens and Zuzanna returns, smiling, holding a bucket of fresh pig's blood.

The trio is quick to gather up the materials for the ritual.

An hour later, as the lamp-lighters appear to begin their nightly rounds, the three companions are making their way into a cordoned area at the corner of South Wallace and West 63rd Streets. No building exists on this street corner anymore; all but the last remnants of the fire-ravaged structure have been removed in preparation for the construction of a replacement building. Even so, Archie swears he can still smell brimstone.

Zuzanna and Archie are able to slip past the ropes easily, but Elspeth is another matter. The ground is soggy with recent rainfall and her wheelchair becomes stuck in the mud. Finally, realizing that they have only moments before a policeman or some concerned citizen sees their trespass, Archie scoops her up from the chair and carries her hastily away. She is twice the weight of a normal woman and he strains beneath her bulk.

Only a few steel walls of the World's Fair Hotel survived the massive blaze three months prior. The newspaper said the walls were part of the horrific gas chambers where H. H. Holmes—a killer possessed by a demon, though that part never appeared in the newspaper—had murdered his victims in perfect secrecy and with terrifying efficiency. Now the strange trio crouch behind these very instruments of murder, hoping the walls are tall enough to conceal their activities from onlookers. Archie lowers Elspeth to the ground and props her against one of the steel walls, hoping that its integrity will hold a little longer.

"Should we wait until night?" Zuzanna asks.

"The magic will be strongest at dusk, I think," Elspeth replies, nodding to the hazy sun just beginning to set over the high rises. "You'll need to start by making a circle with the blood."

"A circle?" Zuzanna repeats.

"On the ground," Elspeth says. "You'll need to seal yourself and all the other tools inside it."

Zuzanna gives Archie a worried glance. He tries to smile in a comforting way, placing his hand on her shoulder. "I'll help you," he volunteers.

The bucket of blood is unwieldy, but Archie manages to pour a ragged circle around Zuzanna. She clutches the bag of spell ingredients to her chest as he does so, her brown eyes huge and doe-like with fear.

Archie squats beside Elspeth and watches

as Zuzanna follows the automaton's instructions to complete the spell. One by one she completes each task, and at some point Archie stops paying attention to the instructions, lost in the pleasure of simply watching Zuzanna move. She is so graceful and elegant, but entirely oblivious to it, which only adds to her charm. When she begins reading the spell, he shuts his eyes to enjoy the cadence of her voice as she speaks the alien language of Elspeth's home world. In the distance carriages rattle past and a lone songbird chirps plaintively.

Suddenly a great gust of wind knocks Archie onto his back. He scrambles to his feet to see Zuzanna floating several feet above the earth. The air crackles with green lightning and smells like rain. Zuzanna's dark hair is whipping about her head in a tangled frenzy, spurred by the powerful wind that seems to blow from everywhere and nowhere all at once. Her eyes glow bright white, beacons in the omnipresent darkness.

"I told you this is her destiny," Elspeth's tinny voice says, full of triumph, barely audible over the ferocious wind.

Archie shakes his head but says nothing. His stomach churns indecisively as the seconds pass. Zuzanna's voice grows louder and more frantic, the wind picks up speed and volume, and the air pressure increases until he thinks his eyes might pop out of their sockets.

"This has gone on too long," Archie finally says, lunging to break the circle of blood.

"No!" Elspeth cries, her vise-like fingers closing around his leg. She's too heavy; he can't move forward with her clinging to him like a lamprey. "You must not stop her now!"

"I have to! She's in danger!" Archie shouts, kneeling and trying to pry the automaton's fingers from his ankle.

"She could die if you interrupt the spell!"

Archie hesitates, eyeing the mechanical woman. With her emotionless features, it's impossible to gauge the truth of her words. Can he truly take the risk that interrupting the spell could harm Zuzanna? Is Elspeth merely lying to keep him in check? Once again paralyzed by indecision, he collapses to the ground.

And then, just as suddenly as it began, the spell ends.

The wind dies down, and the darkness recedes. The normal Chicago night returns, dotted with street lamps and softly glowing windows, bringing with it the usual sound of carriages clattering along the pitted roads. Somewhere, an amorous toad croaks a love song.

Zuzanna has fainted. Archie rushes into the circle without asking permission, gathering her limp body into his arms. Her skin is so much paler than it should be, so much paler and cooler.

"She will recover," Elspeth says from outside the circle, where she struggles to sit upright again.

Archie ignores her; his attention is only for Zuzanna.

A bright light appears beside him, like a lantern's flickering flame. It blinks several times and bounces up and down, as if trying to capture his attention. Archie clutches Zuzanna to his chest to protect her from this strange intruder.

"Have no fear, this creature is of our summoning," Elspeth says. She has managed, with great difficulty, to pull herself upright and to a standing position. She gestures to the light and says a few lilting words in her native tongue.

The light bounces once and then begins to move slowly away.

"We have little time! We must follow," Elspeth says, gesturing to the will-o-the-wisp impatiently. One of her legs flails, and then the other, and she begins following the ball of light in her slow, awkward, halting gait.

"But Zuzanna . . ."

"Bring her if you must, only come quickly!"

Archie doesn't know what else to do, so he obeys, gathering the unconscious woman into his arms and lifting her. After holding Elspeth's metal weight, Zuzanna seems light as a down pillow, insubstantial and soft.

The streets of Chicago are still busy even after dark, but the ball of light guides Elspeth and Archie through clusters of pedestrians and even intersections teaming with carriages. Everyone pauses and watches the light, their pupils growing huge and their mouths slack, until it has passed, and then they return to walking or driving as if nothing had happened. The street grows silent for a few moments as the will-o-the-wisp and its followers make their way through, and then all the hubbub and bustle resumes, as if everyone were briefly hypnotized.

The walk is a considerable one, however, taking them across several wide city blocks before finally hovering near a huge, well-lit mansion. Archie is growing exhausted by the time they stop; Zuzanna is delicate but he is not a strong man, nor young.

With a final bob, the light flickers out.

"Is this it?" Archie asks, looking for a place to deposit his burden.

"Aye. How does Miss Uritski fair?" Elspeth asks, glancing back at her companions for the first time.

"Still unconscious. I should take her back to the hotel."

"We have no time. The demon is here."

"What?! Where?!"

The automaton gestures languidly at the enormous house. "Where did you think our friend was taking us?"

Archie finds a park bench on the street opposite the house, gently settling Zuzanna there, and turns back to Elspeth with a frown. "We're hardly prepared to battle him here, at this moment!"

"When, then?" The mechanical woman demands, her huge eyes gleaming in the light of the nearby street lamp. "When will have another opportunity?"

Archie can't think of a response. While he contemplates, a man appears on the street. He's an ordinary enough fellow, but something about the way he walks strikes Archie as odd. There's a familiar wrongness about him as he makes his way to the front door of the house and rings the bell.

"The demon," Elspeth says.

"How can you be sure?" Archie asks, disliking the way his stomach is convulsing.

"Your reaction. How does your gut feel?"

"What if you're wrong? What if my gut's wrong?"

Elspeth makes no reply. They watch in silence as a butler answers the door and invites the man inside the house. Archie's stomach cramps painfully.

"Fine. Let's go," Archie says, with one backward glance at Zuzanna, carefully laid out on the bench, pale and still as a porcelain doll. "Let's be quick."

The pair make their way to the house with great determined strides. At the door, Archie is reaching for the bell when they hear a gunshot and then the sounds of a tussle. Without hesitation, Elspeth throws open the door and barges into the foyer.

The man from the street is standing in the foyer, a pistol leveled directly at Elspeth's chest. The butler is crumpled on the floor at his feet.

"Hello again, old friend," the man says through gritted teeth.

In a room beyond the foyer, a woman shrieks, high and sorrowful. Archie fingers the pistol in his pocket, but can't get a clear shot with Elspeth blocking his view.

"What have you done this time?" Elspeth asks, her voice ringing in Archie's ears.

The man laughs, revealing crooked yellow teeth. "This Prendergast fellow just had to kill the mayor before we could move on to do more important work. So now he's dead, and I can finish what I started."

"Finish?" Elspeth cries, sounding alarmed.

"Have I said too much?" the man replies.

With a malicious sneer, he pulls the trigger.

Elspeth's chest explodes in a horror of flesh and metal. Her body slumps back against Archie and he barely catches her, the weight bearing them both to the floor; his head contacts the door as he falls, causing him to briefly see bright white against blackness.

When he regains his composure moments later, the demon is gone, and Elspeth's metal form is heavy atop his legs. Heavy and motionless.

Terror welling up in him and making his nerves buzz, Archie pushes Elspeth off his lap and then gathers her in his arms, as he had done with Zuzanna only an hour before. The automaton's face holds no tension, her eyes rolling lazily in either direction, no longer controlled by the soul that once possessed the metal body. Horror washing over him in waves, Archie looks down at her chest to see that the bullet pierced the fabric of her gown, the metal of her skin, and, beneath that, the organs so carefully preserved in Elspeth's chest cavity.

A keening sound issues from his throat

before he can stop it. He rocks back and forth with the heavy automaton held against his chest, great sobs wracking him, looking down at beautiful Betsy's face—once again dead, once again stolen from him too soon.

And what is to become of him now? The demon has defeated them. He and Zuzanna are both doomed without Elspeth to guide and protect them.

Zuzanna.

Archie drops the lifeless automaton and scrambles to his feet. He runs haphazardly into the street, narrowly avoiding a passing motorcar, rushing to the bench where Zuzanna should be resting.

Should be, but isn't. The bench is empty.

Archie looks desperately around for any hint of where she might have gone and by what power. Did the demon carry her off, or did she simply wake, disoriented, and wander away? He sees nothing helpful, not even a footprint, and sits down on the bench with his head between his hands to think.

His mind feels as if it's operating with singular clarity, but it takes him several moments to notice that a police wagon has pulled up to the mayor's house. Several officers clamber down and trundle into the house; one exclaims upon sight of the automaton's corpse sprawled in the doorway.

Archie realizes that, at any moment, the officers will start casting about for witnesses and suspects. With one of his own automatons canted in the foyer—and a pistol in his pocket—Archie is likely to be arrested. He's tempted to return to his suite at the Hyde Park Hotel, where a bottle of bourbon waits to drown his misery. His down comforter calls to him.

"The police will find you in your hotel, and if you are arrested, who will rescue Miss Uritski?" Elspeth asks.

The voice is so clear and sharp that Archie looks around in panic, thinking that the automaton is somehow standing beside him. He is, to his distress, still alone.

"But how will I find Zuzanna?" he demands of the bodiless voice.

There is no reply, but a thought occurs to him. What became of the flickering will-o-the-wisp? It led him once to the demon . . . could it do so again?

Archie hurries away from the mayor's house with his hands thrust in his pockets, trying to appear like a neighbor out for a casual stroll on a cool Autumn night. As he walks, he says a quiet prayer under his breath: "Little friend, little light, please return to me! I need your help to find the demon. You did it once before; please, help me do it again." He repeats these words like a mantra as he shuffles along the sidewalk. No wind blows, no magic tingle indicates that the words are summoning anything. He grows frustrated but keeps reciting the phrase, unable to think of any other solution.

Finally, a tiny light flares to life beside his shoulder. Archie lets out a cry of surprise and relief. The will-o-the-wisp bobs once, as if in greeting. The flame is small and flickering now, as if losing potency. "I need your help to find the demon," Archie says, and the ball of light takes off down the sidewalk with remarkable alacrity.

Archie chases after it. This time, the light's magic is fading, and the traffic doesn't stop for its passage. Pedestrians swat the flame as they would an annoying insect. Archie is forced to shove people aside and run through dangerous intersections to keep up with it.

Eventually the wisp—growing dimmer and rushing faster with each passing moment—stops in the industrial district near the water. The streets here are virtually abandoned, the lamps further apart and the shadows deeper and longer. The wet, musty smell of the lake is strong so close to the shore. The tiny flame rests for a moment before a warehouse building, then fades and disappears into oblivion.

Panting, Archie conceals himself behind an oil drum while he catches his breath. The night seems very dark and forbidding without the hovering light. For the first time in months, he's alone, without Elspeth or Zuzanna to help him decide what to do next. Loneliness and despair threaten to choke him.

Resolving to do whatever he must to rescue Zuzanna, Archie touches the pistol in his pocket, taking comfort from its metal weight.

Light pours from the warehouse's windows two stories above the ground. An inspection of the outer perimeter reveals only one entrance. Reluctantly, afraid of heights but determined not to abandon Zuzanna, Archie pushes oil drums together and stacks them until they're high enough that he can climb them and peer in the high windows. The stack of drums is rickety and the climb horrifying. He spends the better part of an hour trying to create a stable pyramid and then crawling up it, standing at last upon the highest oil drum on his toes, just barely able to see into the windows.

The factory below is ablaze with hundreds of electric lights. Archie blinks against the glare before his eyes are able to focus on the panorama. An enormous machine—obviously cobbled together from junkyard parts, constructed as much from rust as from metal—fills the space like a coiled metal dragon. Great gusts of steam blast from the pipes along the beast's back; giant gears grind and squeak. Squinting through the steam, Archie can make out people gathered around the machine's "head", clustered together as if in conference.

A strong breeze off the nearby lake threatens to topple Archie from his perch; he clings to the window frame until it passes. The wind clears some of the steam out of the factory, briefly giving him an excellent view of the people gathered on the factory floor.

The group are all men, of varying ages and classes; a few are mere boys. Some move through the warehouse with purpose, as if busy on important errands, while others stand around staring at nothing, their faces empty and stupid. One group of fellows, however, stand around a chair, and in the chair, with straps holding her arms . . . Zuzanna, her head lolling to one side, still unconscious.

Archie cries out involuntarily. It isn't apparent what the chair's purpose might be or why Zuzanna is confined there, but he knows with terrible certainty that she is doomed. While he watches in horror, the man who killed Elspeth, still sneering, places some kind of vise over Zuzanna's head, affixing it upon her temples, and then pulls a lever.

The great metal beast shudders and screams as its gears begin to turn. Steam billows from its exhaust pipes, obscuring Archie's view completely. He scrambles down his pyramid of oil drums and hits the ground hard, twisting his ankle. Limping, he makes his way to the door of the warehouse, all the while arguing with himself about whether he should flee. He's walking into an army of the demon's servants, it seems; how can he possibly survive?

Then he thinks of Zuzanna: her sweet voice, her graceful hands, her wide brown eyes . . . and ultimately, he can't leave her.

When he throws open the warehouse door, pistol clutched in his right hand, Archie expects to be rushed by the demon's minions. Instead, the men working in this bizarre factory barely take notice of him; a few look up from their work, but most simply continue doing whatever incomprehensible tasks they were already doing. For some this means continuing to stare blankly at the wall or floor. Others seem to be sorting items, carrying huge pieces of machinery, or wandering about without any clear purpose.

He recognizes one of these: the demon's minion Pietzel, shuffling back and forth across the factory without apparent purpose, his beady eyes focused on the concrete floor. As Archie watches, a droplet of drool escapes the man's open mouth and drips slowly from his lip to the ground. Though the man was always the demon's pet, and therefore evil, something about seeing him this way is horrifying and makes Archie shiver, raising the hairs on his arms. What has become of this once-cognizant man?

Archie makes his way slowly into the factory, leaving the door behind him open so that he might make his escape. Ahead, the machine chugs and screams, rusty gears grinding against one another in a horrible cacophony. The sound makes Archie wince, and he wonders how the assembled men can stand the unbearable screeching.

Finally he approaches the head of the machine, where Zuzanna is strapped into the chair. Her body is rigid and convulsing in the vise that grips her temples. Froth appears on her lips.

"Get away from her!" Archie screams, brandishing the pistol at the demon and his underlings.

The demon-possessed man laughs, a sinister sound, all huge yellow teeth behind dark lips. "What will you do with her?"

"Take her home," Archie says. He points the gun at the demon's chest, threatening to shoot him where he shot Elspeth.

"You can't. She's not yours anymore. Now she's mine."

As the demon speaks, the machine finally shudders to a halt, one last great gust of steam spilling from the exhaust pipes and rising to the windows to escape into the night air. Zuzanna's rigid body relaxes, and she opens her eyes.

She blinks once, twice, three times, and then smiles. She says something in a language Archie doesn't recognize. He feels his heart clench tight in his chest.

He's too late.

The demon says something to the woman who was once Zuzanna. She turns and regards Archie with Zuzanna's eyes, chocolate brown, which once had looked upon him with affection.

She laughs, a sound deeper and more feral than any Zuzanna would make. She says something in the demon language, "Ushara neama shothray," and though Archie can't comprehend the words, he understands the malice behind them.

He turns and runs, ignoring his painful ankle. The night air hits his face and the cool darkness envelopes him. He runs three blocks before he dares to stop and look back; no one has followed.

Archie finds a pub and slinks inside, making his way to a dark corner. He orders bourbon but his hands are shaking too much to hold the glass, so it sits on the table. He stares at it for at least an hour, his mind turning over the night's events again and again. Full of regret, he imagines how differently things would have turned out had he pushed Elspeth aside and killed the demon with a shot from his trusty pistol. What if he had charged into the factory heroically and rescued Zuzanna before she was placed in that awful chair? He still hears the words she spoke in that demonic voice, "Ushara neama shothray," and the alien sounds taunt him.

Finally, his thoughts beginning to make sense again, he rises from the table and leaves a few coins for the barkeep. He stumbles into the street and gazes forlornly back the way he had come, toward the lake, toward the industrial district, toward the factory where the demon was busy making more demons. Archie knows with devastating certainty that the demon is stealing bodies and creating an army of his kind. This is the project that he has struggled to complete for hundreds, maybe thousands of years; this is the apocalypse Elspeth struggled to prevent.

And now, thanks to Archie's cowardice or incompetence, it is coming to fruition.

Archie considers where he can go now. His bed in the Hyde Park Hotel is tempting, as is spending the night in a drunken stupor. He remembers an opium den where once he found sweet oblivion after Betsy's death. He contemplates throwing himself into the lake.

The demon is creating an army. The only way to fight an army is with an army. The only person who knows what the demon plots, the only person who can stop him, is Archie.

The world is doomed, Archie thinks, if he is its only savior. Nonetheless, his feet begin to carry him on a familiar route, taking him back toward the lake, toward the glorious white buildings of the Columbian World's Fair. He goes toward the only place where he can find an army . . . or build one.

He goes toward his destiny.

PART 3

Archie

The Chicago winter is cold and white, the buildings and streets obscured by a steady, relentless snowfall that chokes the city and brings all traffic to a halt. All traffic, that is, except one lone figure, a black silhouette against the stark white.

The figure resolves itself into a man wearing a long coat, a bowler hat pulled low over his ears. He holds something against his chest, wrapped in his coat—something large and unwieldy that his fingers struggle to grip under the thick wool. He wears no gloves, and his bright pink fingers are rapidly giving over to alabaster.

He hurries along the sidewalk—or what must be the sidewalk, though it is now indistinguishable from the street—with purposeful strides, watching his feet as he tramps the snow flat, leaving footprints that in moments will be obliterated. He ducks down an alley and shuffles to a door. Peeling his frozen fingers from the edges of the object he clutches, he manages to tap his knuckles on the steel door, three sharp raps in quick succession and then two slower knocks.

After a few moments, the door is hauled open by a gangly youth. The man rushes inside with a sigh of relief as the boy pushes the door shut behind him.

"I got it," the man says between chattering teeth.

"Well done, Professor Campion!"

"Take it, take it."

The boy reaches into the older man's coat and pulls out a large rectangular object wrapped in oil cloth. He staggers a little under its weight and drops it onto the nearest work bench.

"Did you forget your gloves?" He rushes back to the professor, taking the older man's hands in his to warm them.

The professor only nods. "It's not important. My fingers will recover."

"Be more careful next time, sir. Your hands are too valuable to be lost to frostbite."

"You've been working with me for four

months, Levi. You needn't call me 'sir' anymore. Call me Archie, will you? All this formality makes me itchy."

Levi smiles, releasing Archie's hands to help him remove his coat. "It just doesn't seem right to call you as an equal, sir."

"You've more than proven that you're as brilliant and capable as any university scholar." Archie takes off his bowler and gives it to the boy. He turns and makes his way to the table, where he lays his hands atop the cloth-wrapped object. "I can hardly believe we have it. I've waited so long. The magic is strongest at dawn and dusk but . . . I don't think I can wait any longer."

Levi appears at Archie's elbow, having deposited coat and hat on pegs near the door. "Are you sure it'll work?"

"Of course not. But we have to try. And if it fails, we'll give it a second go at dawn. Then again at dusk, and again, for however long it takes."

With stiff fingers, Archie peels back the cloth to reveal a huge, leather-bound Bible. He opens the cover and reverently runs his fingers over the illuminated vellum pages.

Levi stares at the book with a hungry expression. "This has to be blasphemy."

"Blasphemy to save the world, son, and don't you forget it." Archie flips the pages to the back, where a creature with the head of a man and the body of a goat has been painted. The devil's flesh is red and its tongue lolls obscenely from its mouth, drooping down its chest. Its raised fingers are twisted into arcane gestures.

Archie turns one more page to reveal the Latin incantations, the words scrawled in ink that has a suspiciously red-brown tinge.

"Do you speak the holy language?" Levi asks.

"Not exactly. But I know enough to muddle through. Get the automaton ready."

"Elspeth?"

The name spoken aloud catches Archie off guard. It's strange, because he's used her name many times before—otherwise, how would Levi know what to call her?—but to hear someone else use it, while he holds in his hands the book that might at last bring life back to her dull features, chokes any words he might wish to say. He nods, mute, emotions overwhelming him.

Archie goes into the back room to retrieve the necessary components: a jar of pig's blood, a pouch of herbs, a charm carved from lightning-struck oak and hung from a length of twine, and a silver dagger. When he returns, he finds that Levi has pushed Elspeth's wheelchair into the middle of the workroom. As always, Archie finds the automaton's lifelessness unnerving. Her emerald eyes stare wherever her face is pointed, empty and glassy.

She's still beautiful, even without skin or hair.

"Put these in her lap, and the necklace about her neck," Archie instructs Levi. "Then pour the blood around her in a circle. And don't step into the circle once it's closed."

Levi nods and does as he's told. Archie worries about the powdered pig's blood. As it turns out, liquid blood will coagulate if not dehydrated, so this was his solution for storing it until he could finally use it. He recalls Zuzanna performing a spell for Elspeth, the coppery scent of the fresh blood as he poured it in a ragged circle around her.

Tears rise to his eyes at the thought

of Zuzanna. He automatically glances at the bourbon decanter on a tray in the corner of the room. It has been empty for weeks but he still longs for the sharp flavor on his tongue, the delightful fogging of his memories the liquor can bring.

The circle complete, Levi screws the lid back on the jar. "What now, sir?"

Archie regains his composure. "Uh, yes. Step back. If this works, it will be quite spectacular." He goes to the book on the work bench, lifts it, and turns back to Elspeth.

The words to the incantation are unfamiliar. He stumbles over the pronunciation, stammers like a schoolboy reading at the front of the class. He curses himself and wishes again for a stiff drink to soothe his nerves, but none is coming. He's out of money, out of time. There is no bourbon, and soon they'll run out of money for either rent or electricity, and the project will be doomed. Though he has resolved not to tell Levi of the dire situation, this may well be the only chance they have.

As he reads, Archie waits for the green lightning, the powerful wind, the scent of ozone, but none of them materialize. He speaks the last few words of the recitation in a hushed, disappointed voice, then closes the book and drops it onto the bench. He sinks down beside it and puts his head in his hands.

"Sir?" Levi joins him on the bench, placing one hand on the professor's shoulder. "What was supposed to happen?"

Archie can't immediately make words to reply. His mind is full of Zuzanna, her rose-water scent and dark eyes, her delicate hands and sweet voice. Without Elspeth, he cannot rescue Zuzanna, and without this spell, there will be no Elspeth.

"Oh, Levi, I've been a fool. Months of work, all for nothing. I've ruined myself, and now . . . " he gestures toward the automaton but cannot bear to look at her.

"Maybe the spell will work at dawn. We'll try it again then, like you said."

"Your enthusiasm is admirable but . . . the truth is, I have no idea what I'm doing. This incantation was a shot in the dark at best. It's hopeless."

The two men sit in silence for a few

moments before Archie mumbles, "My life has been dedicated to Elspeth's resurrection for so long that there is little else I can imagine doing. I suppose I'll have to leave Chicago . . ."

A soft click makes them both look up, startled. The automaton is still seated in her wheelchair, but her doll-like eyes are staring directly at Archie and Levi, green irises glittering.

Her eyelids come down as she blinks. Click.

"Elspeth?" Archie whispers.

The automaton's jaw works and a tinny voice issues from her mouth. "Professor Campion."

Archie jumps up and runs to the wheelchair, scuffling through the powdered blood circle and throwing himself at the automaton's feet. "You're back! It worked! You're back!"

"Where am I?" Elspeth's voice is clear and piercing, but flat and emotionless, betraying no confusion or any other feeling. She blinks at Archie, and though he knows it's impossible, he can see the life behind her eyes, the soul looking out at him once more.

"You're in a warehouse! We brought you

here to rebuild your body." Archie dashes the tears from his eyes and gestures to Levi, who steps a little closer, though still not within arm's reach of the mechanical woman. "This is Levi Warner, my assistant."

Elspeth's eyes flick from Archie to the boy and back to Archie. "Where is Miss Uritski?"

Archie hesitates. "She was taken, I'm afraid."

"By the demon?"

"Yes."

The automaton bows her gleaming copper head. "I am sorry to hear that. My condolences, Professor."

"No, no! She's not dead."

"How?"

"The demon built a machine that inserts the souls of his cohorts into the bodies of unwilling victims. Zuzanna is now one of the possessed. But now that you're here, we can free her!"

Elspeth raises one of her hands to her face, studying her fingers. "I look . . . different."

"I dispensed with your polymer flesh. It was impractical."

"Y-your hair, too," Levi stutters.

"I suppose a paladin has little need of shining auburn tresses."

Archie exchanges an incredulous look with Levi. "Was that a joke?"

"How many of the possessed are there now?" Elspeth asks, placing her palms on the armrests of her chair and slowly heaving herself to her feet.

Archie leans in to help her, but ends up hovering ineffectually as the automaton stands without his aid. "We don't know," he confesses. "Dozens, hundreds, more. There could potentially be thousands by now but . . . "

"Has your great city been plunged into perpetual darkness? Do the streets run red with the blood of babes murdered in their beds?"

"Violent crime has become worse than normal since the demon began his work, but no, no rivers of blood."

"Then it's unlikely there are thousands." Elspeth takes a lurching step, then another. "This body is an improvement. My joints no longer stick." She looks up at her creator. "What happened to me?"

"Shot with a pistol, by the demon, when you confronted him. You don't remember?"

Her eyelids lower a little. "I remember a loud bang, and then falling into blackness. And then the void—the space between physical forms." She resumes pacing around the wheelchair in a circle, growing more confident with each step. Finally she stops and looks at each of the men in turn, and says, in her clear, ringing voice, "You have both done well with the improvements to this mechanical body, but I fear that alone, I will be of little use against the demon and his minions. Even with your help, he has superior numbers."

A broad smile curves Archie's lips, and he can't help but twirl his moustache with pleasure. "Never fear; we've done a lot of work these four months. The demon has an army, and so to fight him, you need an army too, wouldn't you agree?"

Elspeth does not reply as Archie takes her arm and guides her into the next room. Levi scrambles ahead of them, lighting a gas lantern and running to ignite others that have been arrayed around the space. This room is larger than the workroom, and crowded with objects, each the height of a man, clustered together and covered with sheets to protect them from dust.

With a flourish, Archie yanks the first sheet away to reveal three automatons, much like Elspeth, only polished steel and brass instead of copper, their heads just as bald and their eyes just as empty as hers had been. Levi unveils the rest, until a dozen gleaming metal women stand before them.

An army. A small one, but with metal skin hardened against ordinary weapons they would be twice as durable as human soldiers.

"How did you do this?" Elspeth asks, her hand going to her chest.

"With ingenuity and money. Lots of money. We've run out, I'm afraid . . . "

"You know that is not what I mean." The automaton's voice is accusatory, her gaze piercing.

Archie frowns and looks at his feet. "Sacrifices had to be made."

"Sacrifices?"

"Only those who were comatose or dying. Their lives were fading. Now, they can benefit the whole human race, a sacrifice many of them would have chosen anyway."

"They were not given a choice?"

"I made the choice for them. A decision had to be made. The demon must be stopped."

"At what price?"

"I would pay any price to get Zuzanna back!" Archie startles himself with the vehemence of his exclamation.

Elspeth steps back from him. She slides her metal fingers into the plate on her chest and pulls. Archie screams for her to stop, but it's too late; she's strong enough that the screws pop and the plate comes free immediately.

The screws clatter to the floor. Inside her chest cavity human organs pulse, red and brown and gray in the lamplight, beating with their own strange, slow rhythm. Elspeth views their reflection in the metal of her chestplate. "To whom did these belong?" Her mechanical voice holds an impossible edge of pain.

"Please, Elspeth, you must see reason. What's done is done. We can't go back now. I made a decision, and we can debate the merits of it later. Now, we need to summon more of your kind to take these automatons so that we can go rescue Zuzanna."

"Miss Uritski is probably past rescuing now."

Archie trembles, hands and voice shaking with the pounding of his heart. "Don't say that! There is always hope. I brought you here to rescue her. I did all this to rescue her! There has to be hope!"

Silence falls over them for a moment as Elspeth considers. Archie follows her gaze as she looks over the heads of her sisters. Some are recognizable from the singing and dancing automaton show that once made Professor Campion famous the world over. This one had worn a Cleopatra costume, that one swung a sword as Joan of Arc, and the third knelt and prayed as Mary Magdalene. Others are new, or pulled from a storeroom, backups in case their sisters failed, at last pressed into service for the greater good.

Elspeth slowly presses the chestplate back in place. "Someone replace the screws, please."

"So you'll do it then?"

Elspeth turns to face her creator. She can make no expression, but somehow she seems disappointed, weary. "Do I have a choice?"

"Levi, get the . . . Levi?" Archie glances about for his assistant. When he cannot locate the boy, he ventures into the workroom again. Levi is nowhere to be found, and neither is the lantern he was carrying. His cap and scarf have disappeared from the pegs by the door.

The Bible with the summoning incantation is gone as well.

"Levi?" Archie rushes to the door, throws it open, and peers out into the night. The cold hits his face with a slap. Between the darkness and the blizzard, any tracks the boy left in his escape are now invisible.

Shivering, Archie pulls the door shut and turns to see Elspeth standing in the workroom. She is surprisingly quiet on metal feet.

"Is there a problem?"

"My assistant . . . he's disappeared." Archie shakes his head, his brow furrowing. His eyes come to rest on the bench where the missing Bible once lay. "He took the book with him, the one with the incantation I used to summon you. Why would he do such a thing?"

"Perhaps to perform his own summoning."

"I don't understand."

"The boy was tainted, Professor."

"He was? But . . . he's worked with me for four months! When I ran out of money he was the only one of my workers who stayed on. He was so industrious, so loyal . . . oh." Archie sinks to the bench, covering his mouth with one hand.

"You are shocked."

"Well of course I am! How was I to know that he was . . . "

"Tainted? You could not have known. I could see it right away. I thought perhaps the boy was a defector."

"A defector?"

"From the demon's camp. Stranger things have happened in this war." Elspeth half-turns toward the workroom. "We should get to work summoning the others immediately. We have much to do, and if young Mister Warner has your book he will no doubt seek to complicate matters."

"And how will we do that? Without the book I can't summon others!"

"The book is not what brought me here, Professor."

Archie stops, blinking. "It wasn't?"

"No. Your will, your drive, your desire . . . and the continued presence of the demon, those are what delivered me back to this place. Remind me of the name of the demon's host?"

"Prendergast. Patrick Prendergast. Here." Archie rummages in a pile of papers and sundries on the floor and pulls out a newspaper dated four months prior. "He shot the mayor, just before he shot you. The mayor of Chicago!"

Elspeth barely glances at the newspaper. "Terrible. Did the police not arrest him?"

Archie jabs a finger at the cover story. "They did! But he escaped. Killed three officers in the process."

"They are lucky they lost only three. The demon is capable of far worse."

Archie swallows hard. "What will we do now?"

Elspeth turns and gestures to the chest plate she yanked free moments before. "Replace this, and then we will summon my sisters, of course."

Archie cannot help but feel some pride as his automatons are brought to life. Elspeth knows the precise incantation to summon souls into his creations, and in only a few hours Archie is sharing the warehouse with thirteen metal women inhabited by the souls of plane-walking paladins.

He feels some sadness that Levi isn't present to witness the completion of their long months of work. The idea that the boy was a traitor, that he lied and deceived Archie for four long months, makes him feel queasy, so he decides not to think about it. Instead, he makes himself useful presenting the warriors with the meager weapons gathered over months of thievery, mostly knives and clubs, and a single machete. He unplugs the automatons from the electrical lines, lubricates stiff joints with oil, tests hearing and eyesight.

Not one of them speaks English, so once they are all gathered, Elspeth translates, explains, and comforts them as they realize the strangeness of their situation. The language of her people is lilting and alien. Archie isn't sure what she's telling them, but the blank stares he receives from their doll-like eyes make him nervous. In their cool regards he sees, for the first time, the immorality of stealing the organs of living people to power inhuman machines. He wants to reason with them, and explain that the lives sacrificed were for the greater good, but he knows the words will be meaningless to their ears.

So he retreats into the workroom, where he loads his pistol with stiff, shaking fingers. He remembers the last time he fired it, into the demon, when it was inhabiting the form of H. H. Holmes—the diabolical murderer—and thinks with regret of how he killed the demon before it could be properly bound into the body. If he had possessed a steadier hand, a surer resolve, they would not be in this situation. Zuzanna would not be stolen from him, and Elspeth could have abandoned her metal form and moved on.

Success in this endeavor is the only way to make that mistake right again. He cannot fail.

Elspeth appears in the doorway. "We are ready."

"How will we bind the demon into his current body?" Archie asks.

"We will do nothing. You will stay here, and your automatons will see the work complete."

"You don't even know where the factory is!"

"I have my ways of finding out. It would speed things along if you just told me, but I can learn the demon's whereabouts without your assistance, if I must."

Infuriated, Archie drops the pistol into his pocket, plants his feet, and gives Elspeth his most determined expression. "I'm going with you. I have to be there."

"Your presence is not required. You will only get in the way."

"I'm going! I'll not discuss it further."

"You seem to think you are in charge."

"I am!" Archie's face is turning red and his eyes are bulging.

Elspeth is cool and robotic. "From the moment I awoke in this body, you have been unnecessary."

"I built you that body!"

"And your involvement ends there."

Archie steps forward, so that he and Elspeth are less than an inch apart, copper and flesh nearly touching. "I'm going."

"I will not lose more human lives

unnecessarily."

Archie doesn't immediately reply, unsure what to do with this statement. With a sigh, he says, "Since Zuzanna was taken . . . I've been dead inside. This work has been my life night and day for four months. I have to see it through." He inhales slowly, but does not step back. "Please, Elspeth, give me that."

Elspeth stares at him unblinking for so long that he starts to think she has vacated her body. "Very well," she finally allows. "But you must remain behind our ranks. I will not have you put in danger if we can prevent it."

Archie pulls on his wool coat and moves to the door. "Let's go."

Elspeth and her metal sisters follow him out into the cold morning. The sun has not yet risen, but the snowfall has slowed to almost nothing, and the bright white that coats every surface reflects the meager lamplight to make the streets strangely bright. The city is quiet except for the occasional crack of an ice-laden branch breaking.

The squadron of automatons moves through this surreal vista, their metal bodies gleaming. They are even more beautiful in motion, and unexpectedly quiet except for the soft hiss of joints moving and the crunching of feet on snow. The blizzard's timing is a blessing. Archie was never quite sure how he would move thirteen metal women through the city without notice, especially when he couldn't even afford to rent a truck. He takes this unexpected blessing as a sign of impending success, and breathes deeply of the cold, clean air, relishing the moments just before what will surely be a victory.

The factory is only a few blocks from the warehouse. Elspeth flicks her hand in a series of quick gestures. The metal warriors nod, softly crunching through the snow as they array themselves around the building. Archie stands back, watching as each automaton moves into position. They are graceful, despite weighing around three hundred pounds apiece, and the snow muffles their footfalls.

They start to chant simultaneously. The sound of their tinny voices raised in the strange, alien language of their home world makes the hair on Archie's arms stand on end. The air pressure increases, and a wind blows from nowhere and everywhere all at once, swirling the snow into a small blizzard around the factory. The chanting builds to a crescendo, until the automatons' voices are lost in the ferocity of the wind.

Green lightning crackles around the building and the air stinks of ozone. The automatons finish their chant, and the wind dies. Elspeth turns back to look at Archie, and gives him a nod.

As one, the metal warriors surge forward. Three of the steel models batter at the factory door. Several others clamber up the walls, nimble as spiders, to break the high windows with brass fists. The sounds of glass shattering and metal groaning disturb the otherwise quiet morning.

The door bursts open and the automatons rush in headlong. Elspeth follows behind them, with Archie close on her heels.

The factory is filled with chaos. Thick gray smoke obscures the view more than a few feet. Demon-possessed men run to and fro, some brandishing weapons, others trying to escape. One with a baseball bat lunges at Elspeth; she backhands him to the floor, where he lays motionless, a pool of blood forming around his head.

"You stay here," she orders Archie.

Stunned, Archie can only nod. Elspeth disappears into the cloud of smoke and violence. Shouted orders, screams, and the sickening crunch of metal fists breaking human bones flood back to Archie where he waits by the door.

He grips the pistol in his pocket so hard that his fingers start to ache. He wonders about Zuzanna. Where is she? Could she be somewhere in the fray? What if one of the automatons accidentally harms her?

After several moments, Archie finally plucks up his courage and rushes forward, calling for Zuzanna. He holds the pistol at his side, ready to raise it and fire at the slightest provocation. The smoke is thick and he immediately starts to cough. He trips over something, looks down, and sees that it is the brass leg of Helen of Troy, one of his favorite automatons. Her face is slack, her chest plate ripped open and the organs within battered into a bloody pulp.

He can distinctly see the wreckage of the automaton despite the smoke, and he realizes that it's clearing. Though the battle itself has moved further into the building, its aftermath becomes increasingly visible. The automatons have decimated the ranks of the demon-possessed, and the bodies of the fallen are abandoned on the floor like the detritus on the beach after a devastating storm. Archie spots only two automatons among the defeated and can't help but feel a little pride at the effectiveness of his glorious metal warriors.

The next emotion he feels is horror. What has he created? The automatons, originally created to entertain, are now efficient machines of slaughter. What if Zuzanna is among those they killed? "Zuzanna!" He calls over the din, hoping she will hear him as he makes his way toward the struggling automatons and men.

"Professor!" Elspeth appears, her copper skin smeared with blood. She clutches a baseball bat in one hand and a machete in the other. "Did I not tell you . . . "

"I couldn't wait! I have to find her! ZUZANNA!"

Elspeth steps forward to say something, but a sudden silence falls in the warehouse, stalling her words. Both she and Archie follow the gazes of those around them to the back of the building.

The smoke has cleared enough that Archie's former assistant, the demon-tainted traitor Levi, is now visible, the stolen Bible propped in one arm and a knife held in his free hand. He has cut his arm and used his own blood to complete the ritual circle on the floor. His skin is pale, the hand holding the knife wobbling as blood continues to flow from the wound.

"Levi!" Archie cries, making a movement to go to the boy.

Elspeth's hand shoots out and grabs Archie's sleeve so hard he stops.

Levi smiles, sighs, and falls, with only the rustle of cloth to mark his passing.

Behind him, something moves in the smog. Something huge, something that groans and screeches and scrapes.

The scrapheap behemoth has only grown in the four long months since Archie last encountered it. Its junkyard body is even rustier and more cobbled together than he remembers, though its cacophony of grinding gears is just as loud. Smoke gusts from the exhaust pipes along its back. It uses welded wreckage arms, tipped with carriage-part claws, to drag itself forward like a half-formed Komodo dragon, its lower half legless and unfinished.

Like a creature out of nightmare, the metal dragon raises its mammoth head. While the collected throng of men and automatons stares, bewildered and horrified, it opens its mouth and prepares to blast them all with its deadly steam breath.

From his perch upon the beast's back, Prendergast laughs with a maniacal cackle.

Zuzanna

Zuzanna is trapped behind her own eyes. She can feel nothing, hear nothing, and see very little. She has only occasional glimpses of the world beyond her prison, in the brief moments when the demon that possesses her is distracted.

The demon is powerful, and full of such seething hatred that it frightens Zuzanna. He squats in her like a toad, slick and heavy and horrible. She struggled in the beginning, when his soul first pressed in upon hers, but he filled her mind with images of exactly what he would do to her—and her loved ones—if she fought him. Unspeakable images.

So she stopped fighting, and retreated as far from awareness as possible. If she cannot stop the fiend from doing what he likes with her body, she can at least refuse to see it. Now all she can do is linger, in sort of a dream-stupor, drifting in and out of awareness as the creature murders and maims and—what is he doing? Building something?

Intrigued, Zuzanna surges forth to look through her own eyes. For a split second she can feel something slippery beneath her hands, smell burning oil, hear the growled commands of the demon's brethren as they labor. They're working on a monstrous machine that breathes smoke and steam, a great metal serpent that seems to have no beginning or end.

Before she can see anything else, the demon shuts her down, locking her out of her own senses. She is relegated back to the darkest recesses of her own mind. In isolation, she worries about Archie and Elspeth. She wonders how long she will be forced to endure this torture before someone kills her and finally releases her miserable soul. Perhaps then she will be free, as Elspeth is free, to find her friends again in another body.

Days, or maybe weeks, pass before she can resurface a second time. The demon is distracted while working on the machine again. This time his efforts are more urgent, almost fevered.

Zuzanna is more cautious now, peering surreptitiously, hoping not to be noticed. The demon is too busy shoveling coal into a burner to pay her any mind. The room is filled with smoke, and she can feel her eyes burning, faintly.

Prendergast. Zuzanna's heart would clench tight in her chest at the sight of the chief demon's current host, if she were connected to it anymore. He issues some order, grins a yellow-toothed smile, and then strides away.

The demon inhabiting Zuzanna is unhappy. She can taste his fear like bile on the back of her tongue. What is Prendergast doing to make his own minions afraid?

The smoke begins to clear. Zuzanna sees a circle of blood on the floor. A boy stands in the circle, a boy possessed as Zuzanna is possessed. He holds a book and a knife. He collapses as Zuzanna watches.

The machine comes to life with a cacophonous grinding of massive, rusted gears.

Zuzanna hears familiar voices shouting and raises her head. Archie and Elspeth. The automaton no longer has skin or hair, but there's no mistaking her determined posture. Zuzanna's heart swells at the sight of her friends, and then clamps tighter than before as she realizes they are staring up at the dragon. It rises above them all like a cobra, poised to strike.

Memories flood Zuzanna's mind, unbidden: welding and bolting sections of the behemoth's metal carapace, shoving fresh organs into the beast's cavities, feeding it coal to keep it alive. The boy, the book, the blood. The ritual.

Archie and Elspeth are in peril. The scrapheap dragon has come to life like Archie's automatons, and is possessed by a soul. Only this soul is evil, this automaton a minion of chaos.

The imminent danger to her friends imbues Zuzanna with new strength. She rushes forward to take back her own senses. The demon grapples with her, but she will not be beaten. Archie's life hangs in the balance! In her mind's eye, she holds down the struggling creature with the pointed toe of one boot, grinding the sole against the demon's neck.

All her senses flood back at once: sight, hearing, scent, even taste. With touch comes pain. Her body aches. The demon has been working it night and day, without rest, for an unknown length of time. Her fingers are caked with filth and her scalp itches. The smoke is acrid and sears her throat. Aware that every moment Archie is in greater danger, she grits her teeth against the pain and looks for him.

"ARCHIE!"

Archie looks up just as Zuzanna barrels into him and pushes him away from the behemoth's open mouth. A blast of steam jets out, narrowly missing his legs.

Elspeth takes the blast without flinching. When the steam clears, she is still standing, brandishing the baseball bat and machete. She stares up at Prendergast with no hint of fear.

Behind Elspeth, the demon-possessed men begin screaming. The heat from the dragon's steam blast is melting the flesh from their bodies. The automatons step back and watch with expressionless faces as the men writhe and cry. Zuzanna looks away from the horror, pressing her face into Archie's lapel.

From the dragon's back, Prendergast shouts a command, willing his mount to attack.

"Zuzanna?" Archie touches her chin, raising her face up to him. "Is it really you?"

"It's me," she says. The demon rages within her, but Zuzanna only presses harder upon it, forcing it down into the dark recesses where she has been forced to dwell for long months.

Archie looks deep into her eyes. "But you were—"

"GET OUT OF HERE!" Elspeth screams at them. She crouches before the behemoth. In one powerful leap, she launches herself at the beast, landing upon its head with all the grace of a descending dancer.

Archie bundles Zuzanna in his arms and moves toward the exit. From over his shoulder, she watches as the automaton army swarms onto the dragon. Elspeth plunges the machete into the beast's shining black eye. It shakes and rears, trying to throw her, but she clings to it with impossibly strong fingers.

Joan of Arc scrambles up one leg to tear at the behemoth's side. Mary Magdalene hacks at its chest with a hatchet. Cleopatra, weaponless, crawls beneath the dragon's belly and begins yanking off the panels that protect its vital organs. The metal women shove gleaming hands into its orifices, punch their way through haphazardly welded panels, and yank out whatever they can.

The monster thrashes and rolls, crushing automatons, flinging them to the walls and floor, clawing at them and biting them with its powerful jaws. Fluids leak from Cleopatra's severed arm. Mary's hatchet still strikes the dragon, though her legs are flattened. Joan's chest is pierced by a jagged metal tooth, her body twisted in the creature's jaws.

But the automatons rise, and rise again, attacking despite the massive injuries. Elspeth climbs up the behemoth's spine toward Pendergast despite the continual danger of being thrown from the writhing monster's neck. She reminds Zuzanna of a cowboy riding a frenzied steer, clinging to his saddle horn with one hand as the bull bucks and kicks.

"Elspeth! Archie, wait!" Zuzanna cries as Archie tries to take her out the door.

Archie turns, and they watch together as Elspeth finally arrives at the top of the behemoth's spine, still gripping the machete. Prendergast is distracted trying to maintain his hold on the shuddering, flailing monster. He throws a kick at an automaton near his perch, issuing curses that are drowned by the beast's screeching gears.

Elspeth is an avenging angel. She leaps, swinging the machete with all the power in her inhuman arms. Prendergast looks up just as her copper form descends upon him, the machete hewing his head in half before he can react.

Zuzanna whimpers, fighting the urge to vomit at the sight of Prendergast's skull split open like a melon. Inside her, the demon writhes with pleasure.

Masterless, the dragon is now unfettered and free to unleash its true fury. Its body heaves, tossing Elspeth—and Prendergast's corpse—off its back, out of sight. Its sinuous tail lashes out and strikes the support columns in the center of the warehouse.

Archie vaults clear of the building, pulling Zuzanna behind him. The dragon's tail pulls hard upon the columns and they begin to crack and groan. The roof splits open, chunks of ice and snow falling in hard, striking the behemoth's superheated metallic frame. The snow is instantly turned to steam, and the dragon is cloaked in a nimbus of white as it rolls and thrashes, bringing the building down upon it and its enemies.

"Elspeth!" Zuzanna screams, trying to turn back. Archie grabs her about the waist and throws her over his shoulder. She doesn't fight him, not wanting to hurt him, and can only watch as the factory collapses in on itself, steel groaning and steam hissing.

A few dozen feet clear of the fallen building, Archie finally deposits Zuzanna on the ground. He sits down beside her, panting, one hand on his chest. His face is red and eyes bloodshot.

"Are you all right?" Zuzanna asks him, suddenly concerned that this excitement is too much for him. He's not a young man.

Archie's reply is interrupted by the sound of snow sliding and concrete cracking. With a crackling, metallic roar, the dragon rears up from the debris of the factory, fixing its one good eye upon Archie and Zuzanna. They can hear its bellows working, the sucking in of breath as it prepares to unleash a torrent of flesh-melting steam in their direction.

Zuzanna is filled with regret. She wishes she had never allowed Archie to rescue her. She should have thrown herself in front of the dragon's deadly breath the moment she had regained control of her body. Then Archie would not have been slowed by carrying her, and he would be well away from here and not in danger.

With a sound half-scream and half-whimper, she throws herself between her beloved and the beast. An explosion rips through the chest of the dragon, fire and steam and chunks of metal engulfing it. Zuzanna flinches away, expecting the blast to sear the skin from her bones. When that doesn't happen, she dares a glance at the behemoth.

The dragon's body is sinking beneath

what remains of the snow-covered factory roof. It lets out a low, shuddering groan as its head sinks out of sight, obscured by fire and smoke.

"Elspeth!" Zuzanna screams, struggling to her feet. What if the automaton is still alive beneath all the fire and smoke and charred metal? She lunges for the factory.

Archie grabs her around the waist with arms that possess surprising strength. "Her body could not have survived that explosion." His head sinks toward his chest. "She's gone, Zuzanna. She's gone."

Zuzanna wails, long and low, and relents to Archie's embrace. Deep within the recesses of her mind, the demon chuckles, a sound like rusty gears grinding.

Elspeth

Chicago in summer is a sharp contrast to the dreary cold of the city in winter. Though her steps carry her on a dark mission, a small part of Elspeth, a part she struggles to suppress, cannot help but enjoy the bright sunlight and friendly, gaily-dressed ladies. But even that small pleasure fades as she makes her way to a small but well-tended townhouse and knocks on the door. She can feel the demon's presence within, but even so, she hesitates; this is her last visit, the final confrontation on her docket, and one she has postponed for a reason.

The door opens. A barrel-chested middle-aged man stands in the doorway, looking startled. She almost doesn't recognize him, as he's trimmed his mustache and gained some silver in his hair since she last saw him. "May I help you?"

Elspeth hesitates again, licking her lips. "Professor Campion . . . Archie." She prepared so many speeches for this moment, rehearsed it in her mind so many times, but these are the only words she manages to stutter.

"Do I know you?"

"Yes, and no," she hesitates and looks away from him. "When you knew me last, I looked very . . . different." She meets his suspicious gaze, hoping that somehow he will know her.

One of his eyebrows raises, but there is no hint of recognition in his face as he examines her wheat-gold hair and pale blue eyes.

"I had hoped you might know me,

despite this flesh-and-blood form."

He shakes his head, considering the impossible. "This can't be."

"It is. You know who I am."

"I most certainly do not. Please leave."

"Professor... Archie." She raises her arm to her heart, imitating the stiff and mechanical way it moved when she was in her automaton body. "It's me, Elspeth."

Archie scowls. "How do I know you're truly Elspeth, and not some impostor?"

"You confessed to me that you were in love with Miss Zuzanna Uritski many months ago, in a hotel not far from here. A woman was struck by an automobile in the road, and you were afraid it was Zuzanna who was injured."

In her imaginings of this moment, Elspeth expected Archie to smile and welcome her in with a warm embrace, eager to reunite with his old friend. But that doesn't happen. Instead he glances left and right of the door, as if assuring himself that no one sees their exchange, and ushers Elspeth inside. She follows him into the foyer and from there, into a small but pleasantly appointed parlor room. The professor closes the door behind them.

"Why are you here?"

"This is not the welcome I had hoped for."

Archie looks embarrassed. "I'm sorry. It's just . . . you died in the battle at the factory. Your automaton was damaged beyond recognition. Zuzanna was heartbroken. She hoped you might reappear to let us know that you were still well. It took me months to convince her to let go of the hope she might see you again. And after all that happened . . ." He shakes his head. "She still has nightmares, you know, about that factory. The demons, the dragon, all of it. I don't want to dredge up the memories we've been trying to lay to rest."

Elspeth sits on the divan, folding her hands neatly in her lap, imitating the most gracious of ladies. "I understand your concern, but I must speak with her."

Archie blinks. "She's unwell. You can perhaps come back some time later but—no, no, I'm afraid that I simply cannot allow you to see her."

"Are you married now then, so that

Zuzanna is your property?"

"She's not my property, but yes, we are married."

"She is your property if you are deciding whom she may see."

"She's my wife. I care about her, and I don't think seeing you will do her any good."

"And what about me, Archie?"

Archie's brow furrows in an all-too-familiar fashion. "What about you?"

"I returned to this world to see Prendergast's demon put to rest, and help you rescue the woman you love. I've returned again because one of Prendergast's minions still roams your world, and I can't leave until all the demons who escaped the factory are exorcised. And there were more than a few, but now only one remains."

"What does Zuzanna have to do with that?"

Elspeth sighs. She had hoped that perhaps he wouldn't be completely obtuse. "She is still possessed."

"She hasn't been possessed for months!"

"The demon is still there, Archie. She's

holding it back with force of will, but it will win out eventually, and you will lose her."

"No, no, no, it can't be. She's my wife. Don't you think I wouldn't know if she were still possessed by a demon?"

"I can sense it. She's upstairs right now, is she not? Just there." Elspeth nods to the corner of the ceiling. "The demon is like a beacon for me."

"How is that possible? You didn't have the ability to sniff out demons before."

"That was in a metal body. Now I have a human one, and my full faculties have returned, including my ability to sense my quarry."

"Your quarry?" The professor's face reddens. "My wife is not an animal for you to hunt!"

Elspeth bows her head. "I'm sorry, I chose my words poorly. It's not Zuzanna I'm pursuing. It's the demon, but unfortunately that demon resides within her body."

"I don't believe it." He looks away from her. One of his hands is shaking with a slight tremor.

"Does she have nightmares? Does she sleep-walk, does she have arguments with herself?"

Archie presses his lips together. "She suffered a great trauma...."

"She's possessed by a demon of the Rusted Vale. It grows stronger each day, biding its time until it can return to full strength. Do you want to die at your wife's hands? Do you truly want that on her conscience?"

"Archie? Is that you I hear?" Zuzanna's voice drifts down from the second floor, muffled by the parlor door. Elpseth's heart unexpectedly lurches in her chest at the sound of it.

The professor pales. "You should leave." He rushes to the back of the parlor and opens the rear door. "Go out through the kitchens."

"Please, Archie. Let me help you before it's too late."

"Go now, before I call the police." His expression is hard and sorrowful.

Elspeth rises and goes to the fireplace. She pulls a calling card from her reticule and lays it on the mantel. She is startled by movement in the mirror above the mantel; she's still not accustomed to the very human face that stares back at her.

"I miss Elspeth sometimes," she whispers. The words are a confession that she has longed to divulge.

"I do, too," Archie admits. "Now please, go."

"When you're ready, please contact me. I'll be waiting."

Archie says nothing as she glides out the door, through the kitchen and out into the back garden.

Elspeth pauses at the garden gate to look back at the house. In the second-story window, she sees Zuzanna. Her hair is a black, tangled cloud, and the hands she presses to the window are smeared with ink or soot. In the sunlight, her eyes are not brown, but rather amber, like molten fire, twin points of bright gold in the otherwise dark window.

Zuzanna nods at her, a slow movement of her head. Elspeth nods back. Neither woman smiles. As Elspeth watches, Zuzanna retreats from the window, disappearing in shadow.

Elspeth smells the scent of rain, and hurries home before the storm can break.

Sarah Hans is an award-winning writer, editor, and teacher. Sarah's short stories have appeared in over twenty publications, but she's best known for her multicultural steampunk anthology Steampunk World. You can read more of her short stories, nonfiction ramblings, and novel chapters on her Patreon for just $1/ month at https://www.patreon.com/sarahhans or find her on twitter at https://twitter.com/steampunkpanda.

Dragon's Roost Press is the fever dream brainchild of dark speculative fiction author Michael Cieslak. Since 2014, their goal has been to find the best speculative fiction authors and share their work with the public. For more information about Dragon's Roost Press and their publications, please visit: http://thedragonsroost.net/styled-3/index.html.

Also Available from Dragon's Roost Press by Sarah Hans

Dead Girls Don't Love

Do you enjoy creepy stories about people who don't quite fit in? Dead Girls Don't Love is a collection of poignant tales for the outsider in all of us.

For a domestic violence victim, there is no life after death--but could there be revenge?

Can a woman returning to her life after 40 years with the fae remember how to be human?

When two Buddhist monks travel to China to spread the dharma, will they survive the unspeakable horror they find instead?

What really happened when the Big Bad Wolf ate the lonely grandmother living in the woods?

Will the love between two zombified women help them break the spell that binds them in eternal servitude?

And, perhaps most importantly, can an Elder God find true love?

Also Available from
Dragon's Roost Press

Hidden Menagerie Vols One and Two

Edited by Michael Cieslak   Edited by Michael Cieslak

Welcome to the Hidden Menagerie -- a collection of
short fiction involving various cryptozoological creatures.
In the first volume you will meet the beasts of the land.
Inside these pages you will be introduced to new visions
of some creatures you are familiar with like the Abomi-
nable Snowman and the Wendigo, creatures long thought
extinct which live on to this day, and others you may have
never heard of.

In the second volume you will meet the beasts of the air,
sea, and animate vegetation. Inside these pages you will
be introduced to new visions of some creatures you are
familiar with like the Kraken, Mermaids, and Lake Mon-
sters, creatures long thought extinct which live on to this
day, and others you may have never heard of.

These volumes contains 35 stories by some of the best
dark speculative fiction writers working today.

A portion of the proceeds from all sales of Hidden
Menagerie Vols 1 & 2 benefits the Lost Day Dog Rescue
Organization.

Also Available from Dragon's Roost Press

Robotic Animals
Televisions Which Reveal Alternate Universes
Inanimate Objects Brought to Life
People Struggling to Survive in Apocalyptic Wastelands
Sentient Cutlery

and much, much more

Desolation: 21 Tales for Tails is a collection of dark speculative fiction whose stories all focus on themes of loneliness, isolation, and abandonment.

Enter into strange worlds envisioned by some of the most inventive writing today.

Combine the mind splintering horror of the Cthulhu Mythos and the heart shattering portion of that most terrible of emotions -- love -- and what do you have? You have *Eldritch Embraces: Putting the Love Back in Lovecraft*.

Some of the best authors working in the fields of horror and dark speculative fiction blends romance and Lovecraft in a way which will make you sigh, smile, weep, or leave you the hollow shell of your former self.

Also Available from Dragon's Roost Press

The Maiden's Courage

by Mary Lynne Gibbs

The best man on the pirate ship is a girl named Alex.

Alexandra "Alex" Gardner is the reluctant cabin boy on *The Bloody Maiden*, a ruthless pirate ship run by the charmingly evil Captain Montgomery. The crew is convinced she's a boy, and she hopes it stays that way until she has the chance to avenge the deaths of her mother and brother at the hands of the crew. All goes well until the ship takes a handsome captive. Could her feelings for him ruin her charade?

Sebastian Whitley is a young man in love. He sails on his father's ship, trying to find the beautiful girl he's lost. When he's captured by *The Bloody Maiden*, the annoying cabin boy saves his life – and makes it more difficult at the same time. His savior is actually a girl, and if Sebastian doesn't keep quiet, it could mean both their deaths.

Together, they have to thwart a mutiny, get revenge, and get off the ship before Alex's secret is revealed. If not, it's the plank for both of them.

Also Available from Dragon's Roost Press

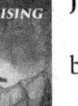 **Jericho Rising**

by Mary Lynne Gibbs

In post-World War III, small town Michigan, a self-proclaimed, violent, and insane High Priestess has taken control, reducing the remaining men to nothing more than slaves and playthings.

Jericho, the reluctant leader of the Resistance, must fight her own family to preserve the freedom and equality of all in her care – male and female alike. She's torn between love and duty, and with traitors around every corner, she has no idea who to trust anymore.

 **Jericho's Redemption**

by Mary Lynne Gibbs

The battle is over, but the war has just begun. Jericho returns to the Obsidian camp, only to learn that her sister Candace destroyed it as part of a plot to dismantle the resistance movement that brought down their mother, the High Priestess. The rest of the resistance blames Jericho for the deaths of their friends, but that's the least of her worries. Not only does Jericho now have to right the wrongs her sister has done, she must contend with a few guests to the camp who bring secrets that will change her life forever. Either she'll redeem herself in the eyes of her comrades, or she'll die trying.

Also Available from Dragon's Roost Press

Hell Hath No Fury

by Peggy Christie

Ever wonder how you might handle a sabbatical from work? Think the bible told you everything there is to know about the Devil? What if the noises coming from under your child's bed weren't just in his imagination? Crack open *Hell Hath No Fury*, a collection of 21 tales of horror and dark fiction, to learn the answers to these questions. Discover stories of psychotic delusions, ghosts, a murder victim's revenge, and a family brought closer together through torture.

Sex, Gore, and Millipedes

by Ken MacGregor

Ken MacGregor, known for pushing boundaries in horror, for shoving the reader outside of their comfort zone, has finally gone too far. *Sex, Gore, and Millipedes* is a collection of the sickest stuff you've ever read. This book will hit your triggers. Hopefully, all of them. You've been warned.